George Birkbeck Norman Hill

Dr. Johnson

His Friends and his Critics

George Birkbeck Norman Hill

Dr. Johnson
His Friends and his Critics

ISBN/EAN: 9783337398705

Printed in Europe, USA, Canada, Australia, Japan

Cover: Foto ©Raphael Reischuk / pixelio.de

More available books at **www.hansebooks.com**

A CRITICAL EXAMINATION

OF

DR G. BIRKBECK HILL'S

"JOHNSONIAN" EDITIONS

ISSUED BY THE CLARENDON PRESS, OXFORD

By PERCY FITZGERALD, M.A., F.S.A.

AUTHOR OF "LIFE OF JAMES BOSWELL"; EDITOR "BOSWELL'S JOHNSON."

LONDON

BLISS, SANDS & CO.

12 BURLEIGH STREET, STRAND, W.C.

MDCCCXCVIII

PREFACE

Naturally I feel some hesitation in putting forward these strictures on Dr Birkbeck Hill's Editions: for has not Mr Leslie Stephen written of "The Life" that "The edition by Dr G. B. Hill is by far the best; the notes throughout are of the highest utility?" ("Dict. Nat. Biog.," vol. xxx. p. 46). And Mr Andrew Lang, has he not declared that, to the same editor we owe "The best edition of Bozzy—the most delightful of books—the best 'Collections of Johnsoniana?'" (*Longman's Magazine, February* 1898, p. 374). Yet how reconcile this eulogium with the incredible catalogue of mistakes, misapprehensions, wild flounderings, and speculations, which are here set forth? With such things present there cannot be "by far the best edition," or even a fairly good one. I do not profess to explain the discrepancy, but leave it to the reader to judge for himself.

February 1898.

CONTENTS

EDITING A LA MODE

OR AN EXAMINATION

OF

DR GEORGE BIRKBECK HILL'S

"JOHNSONIAN" EDITIONS

THE PREFACE AND DEDICATION.

SOME ten or eleven years ago, the Clarendon Press took up the project of an issue of Boswell's "Life of Johnson," to be edited by Dr G. Birkbeck Hill, of Pembroke College. No expense or trouble was spared. The work was fifteen months in passing through the Press; *carte blanche* was given to the editor for illustrations, *fac-similes*, etc.; and the six handsome volumes at last emerged from the Press, finely printed, on fine paper, in "roxburghe binding." Here was the long-expected final edition of "Boswell," and the critics expatiated on the research, the labours, and the ingenious "discoveries" of the laborious editor. "A literary monument," said one, "which will stand for ages." "The classical edition, the scholar's Boswell," said another. This, however, was transcended by the burst in the *Daily News*. "*Six volumes of solid happiness!*" None of these, perhaps, knew exactly what was classical, or what would "stand for ages." Stranger was it that not a single blemish or error was pointed out! Even that accomplished and careful critic, Mr Leslie Stephen, was beguiled into giving the high testimonial that he thought it the best edition he knew of.

In the face of these lavish praises, I propose in this book to challenge seriously the editor's claims; to prove that his system is radically wrong, and that his work teems with mistakes, misconceptions, delusions, and with "discoveries" that are purely imaginary. This is a grave indictment, but I think it will be supported. These defects may be owing to a too ardent enthusiasm, inordinate hurry, or, it may be, to an exaggerated confidence in his own powers or knowledge of the subject.

Dr B. Hill, while he professes to execrate the memory of "the inventor of the preface" (whoever he was), himself rather comically furnishes a preface of monumental cast—a perfect unique—the longest perhaps on record, stretching to nearly twenty closely-printed pages. It is mainly about the editor himself: his early life and education, his joys, sorrows, and illnesses, with very little about Boswell. At the end he is so carried away that he almost comes to think of it as his own work. "*My book* has been my companion," etc. "*My* proof sheets," etc. Even the dedication is a curious thing. It is addressed to the late Master of Balliol, Dr Jowett, and is arranged thus oddly:

"WHO IS NOT ONLY

"AN ACUTE AND KNOWING CRITIC,

"BUT ALSO

"JOHNSONIANISSIMUS,"

Which suggests one of young John Chivery's epitaphs on himself. "The Master" must have smiled at the impressive "*But also*," and at his being dubbed "a *knowing* critic." Nor was he likely to have accepted "Johnsonianissimus," which seems a wrong form, being an English adjective, and not, as it should be, an English proper name, Latinised. The positive should be "Johnsonus," and the superlative "Johnsonissimus," not "Johnsonianissimus."

Dr. B. Hill actually extracted a promise that he would read all "my proofs"—but here "the Master" showed himself a very "knowing critic," and, as our editor very frankly tells us, "after he had seen a few of the sheets, *he confessed he was satisfied*."

ARRANGEMENT AND LAYING OUT OF THE WORK.

BOSWELL'S original title-page, professed to be reproduced here, is misleading, and a misdescription: "Boswell's Life of Johnson, including Boswell's Journal of a Tour to the Hebrides, and Johnson's Diary of a Journey into North Wales." Boswell's "Life of Johnson" does *not* include either of these things. His "Journal" was a separate work, and with the "Diary" he had nothing to do. A most serious blemish is the arrangement of the notes. When a work of this kind is illustrated with additions and comments by another "hand," such matter should, of course, be marked with the writer's name, so as to distinguish them from the author's. Here, strange to say, Dr B. Hill's numerous notes are unsigned, and, at first sight, appear to be the legitimate notes of the text: while we find every one of Boswell's notes marked "Boswell," as though he were some intruder or outsider. A man in his own house has no need to label his property with his name; if anything be labelled, it should be the effects of strangers. Malone, when preparing the third edition, was careful to mark every additional note by brackets and initials. Mr Croker marked all his own very voluminous notes, "Croker." But Dr B. Hill even thrusts passages of his own composition into Boswell's notes, and thus spoils their symmetry. Boswell, for instance, furnished a business-like list of Johnson's residences: "1, Bolt Court; 2, Gough Square; 3, Johnson's Court," etc. This becomes, under our editor's treatment: "17 Bolt Court, No 8 (he was here on March 15, 1776, *ante* II. 427). From about 1765 (*ante* I. 493) to Oct. 7, 1782 (*post*) he had, moreover, an apartment at Streatham." But Boswell was speaking of *London* residences. We must doubt, too, the propriety of introducing a headline over every page of the editor's composition, which affects to describe the subject-matter of each page. This was not, at all events, Boswell's idea. Another adornment which shows a lack of delicate instinct, is the supplying an elaborate modern engraved map for the "Tour." Now, Boswell gave a very clear outline map, without any shading of mountains, etc.—a plan or diagram of the "Tour," as it were, which has a quaint, antique look. This should surely have been reproduced. Again, Boswell, in all the titles of his "Tour," seemed to pride himself on a piquant little device, which he had specially engraved, his crest, a hawk, and motto, "*Vraye foy.*" This is missing in Dr B. Hill's edition. Boswell also gave *fac-similes* of Johnson's writing at different periods of his life, which he placed on a single page for convenience of comparison. But Dr B. Hill supplies various huge *fac-simile* letters at full length, which have to be folded and refolded and unfolded, often double pages, and give a clumsiness to the volume. It is the same with the subjects of the many fine prints which are introduced, but after a capricious principle.

Then the appendices offer a strange "renovation of hope" with perpetual disappointment. A whole "section" is thus introduced as promising something highly important, with this title:

"*Boswell's intention to attend on Johnson in his illness, and to publish 'Praises of him.'*"

Now, this seemed to hold out something novel. But we only find this extract: "I intend to be in London in March, chiefly to attend on Dr Johnson with respectful attention. I intend to publish," etc. Such is the entire section.

Another long appendix is devoted to an account of George Psalmanazar and his character. Other remarkable, curious, and eccentric personages alluded to in the text might have equal claim to this separate form of treatment. But will any one guess what was our editor's reason for selecting Psalmanazar? Not the importance of the adventurer; not the editor's own judgment, but this: "I have complied with the request of an unknown correspondent ('query, anonymous'), who was naturally interested in the history of that strange man." The mysteriousness is extraordinary. Granting that the unknown one was "naturally interested," was his "request" therefore to be attended to?

The last of the six great volumes is almost entirely devoted to indexes and abstracts. It is, indeed, a perfect "curio" in its line. Thus, we unfold what looks like a weather map, a strange mystery or diagram, with crossed lines, and figures, and colours, and columns, which is described as, "*A chart of Dr Johnson's Contemporaries, drawn up by Margaret and Lucy Hill, on the model of a chart in Mr Ruskin's 'Ariadne Florentina.'*" *Diable!* Recovering from this we pass on to: "Titles of many of the Works quoted in the Notes," filling twelve closely-printed pages. Of "many," but why not all? If they are "quoted in the notes," they are only at the particular place. Why have them over again here? Next we come upon what is called "Addenda," scraps from a number of Johnson's letters—which, it seems, were sold at Sotheby's some years ago, all more or less trivial—such as an account of "Young Strahan at College," having no relevancy to Boswell's "Life of Johnson," where Dr B. Hill wanders off on his own account with "My friend, Mr C. J. Faulkener, Fellow and Master of University College, has given me the following extracts"—which are concerned with the election of the young George Strahan to the

Bennett Scholarship! This leads on to a disquisition on the value of the Bennett Scholarship in 1764—how much was the emolument, etc. Next we come to an index of these "Addenda"; and then to the gigantic general index, which consists of no less than 288 pages, or nearly 600 columns! It has indexes within indexes—indexes to Johnson's and Boswell's lives, to Scotland, Ireland, etc. Yet another index follows, oddly denominated "Dicta Philosophi," or a concordance of Johnson's sayings; with a third. We may contrast with this bulk Mr Croker's simple, admirable index, which fills not quite thirty pages.

Surely a writer so enthusiastic, so familiar with his subject, ought to know the exact name of the first published production of James Boswell. His index proves that he has never seen it—certainly never read it. In it we find a reference in italics to "*The Club* at Newmarket." Turning back to the text it is there again, "The *Club*," etc. Now, Boswell had indeed written a piece "The *Cub* at Newmarket," and it will be urged that this was a mere slip, or printer's error, "Cub" and "Club" being so like. But it goes deeper than this. "The Cub" was a piece of doggerel in which Boswell foolishly applied the term "Cub" to himself, so the title exactly described his own "antics." It was no misprint. This production is never alluded to in Boswell's own work, and indeed is little known, but it is found in the letters to Temple, where it is also misprinted "Club," and that misprint it was that misled the editor.

After all this labour, the editor tells us he "will be greatly disappointed if actual errors are discovered" in his index. But we have found some of reference, paging, etc., and he himself confesses that though, under the headings of America, Oxford, London, Ireland, etc., he sets out all that falls under such heads, somehow "the provincial towns of France, by some mistake, I did not include in the general article." The following is grotesque enough. Under "Port," we have, "it is rowing without a port, *i.e.* without an object;" on which the editor refers us, *see* "Claret."

We turn to "Bute," and find:—"BUTE, third Earl of, Adams, the architect, patronises, II. 325." This seems an odd sort of "Pigeon" English. Adam, by the way, and not Adams, is the architect's name. Some of the Johnsonian dicta are not Johnsonian at all, and would appear to have slipped into the list from the general index. Thus we have Cibber's old jest about the pistol missing fire; and under "*quare*," "A writ of *quare adhæsit pavimento* (*Wags of the Northern Circuit*), III. 261," which refers to the well-known hoax upon Boswell. We have also Mrs Salisbury's sayings, with the one about "No tenth transmitter of a foolish face," etc.; and finally the quotation—"Live pleasant, *Burke;*" with Quin's and Lord Auchinleck's speeches about kings, and "Boswell's description of himself as 'Baro,'" all which are classed as "sayings of Johnson."

I suppose, if we were to search all the known indexes, we should never find one in which the pronoun "I" is entered and referred to with chapter and verse. Our editor has actually done this feat. Here it is, with chapter and verse. In the index to the "Dicta Philosophi" we find the letter "I" set down by itself; then follows this reference: "*I* put my hat upon my head, II. 136, *n.* 4"! We rub our eyes, but there it is! And this doggerel, moreover, is one of the "Dicta Philosophi"—one of "Johnson's strong and pointed utterances" which the editor has collected for the "literary man"! Another of these "strong and pointed utterances" we find under the word "Hog"—"Yes, sir, for a hog."

The strangest of Dr B. Hill's delusions is that

he "fondly thinks" that Dr Johnson "would have been *proud* could he have foreseen this edition." What! an edition in which he is attacked, accused of inconsistencies in every page—even of corrupt practices—and in which he is now rebuked, now patronised by Dr B. Hill! So far from feeling pride, he is more likely to have dealt with the editor as he once dealt with Osborne, the bookseller. Surely all who read these notes will be struck by the determined way in which the editor criticises or confutes opinions of Johnson by introducing passages from his writings which are opposed to these opinions Yet at the end he has the strange confidence to declare that *he has never "thought it his duty to refute or criticise Johnson's arguments."* When the sage says anything, there is sure to be a perpetually recurring "yet": *Yet* he did, or said, or wrote so and so, and was therefore inconsistent. Nay, Dr B. Hill fantastically bids any one who would be rash enough to think of doing such a thing "to place Johnson's portrait *after Reynolds*" (but *which* portrait after Reynolds?) "before him, and reflect that if the sage could rise up and meet him face to face he would be sure, on whatever side the right might be, if the pistol missed fire, to knock him down with the butt-end of it." In such case it would go hard with our editor.

Finally, he assures us that "When Edmund Burke witnessed the long and solemn procession entering the Cathedral of St Paul's, as it followed Sir Joshua Reynolds to his grave," he was certain that it would have gratified the deceased painter, for he was not indifferent to such "observances." This is the editor's method of proving, by a figure, that Johnson and Boswell would both have been delighted with this edition, and the printing of the work by the Clarendon Press. Indeed, our editor is so eager to secure approbation for his work that he insists on interpreting the feelings and sentiments of the illustrious dead. He tells us, with much complacency, that as Johnson was "so deeply attached to his own college, he would not have been displeased to learn that his editor had been in that once famous nest of 'singing birds.'" Dr B. Hill is not his editor, on this occasion at least. It seems a rhetorical flourish. Stranger still, the editor fondly thinks, "that of Boswell's pleasure I cannot doubt," *i.e.* a pleasure at having his work pulled to pieces, overburdened to extinction almost with notes and comments, every second statement challenged, flouted, contradicted, laughed at—his whole book re-arranged! It was enough to make him shed tears.

But then the work was done by an Oxford man, was printed in Oxford, and all that came from Oxford, or was of Oxford, would have a special charm for "Bozzy"! An amazing delusion this—for Boswell was not an Oxford man at all, and only visiting it occasionally. "How much he valued any tribute from Oxford is shown by the *absurd importance* he gave to a sermon preached by Mr Agutter," the performance being so contemptible that it could only have been admiration for Oxford that permitted him to admit it. But what is the fact? Boswell was enumerating minutely what he calls the "accumulation of literary honours," which were heaped on his friend after his death, among which was the high compliment of a sermon in memory of Johnson, preached before the University. Could he with propriety have omitted such an honour? The mention of it, and the quotation from it, is simply historical, and had nothing to do with any personal liking for Oxford.

The argument, such as it is, completely fails, and to it the editor has given "an absurd importance."

THE EDITOR'S "EDITING."

THE charm of a well edited book is always more felt than described. The scrupulous editor —who is judicious and restrained by his reverence for his author—seems to glide about noiselessly; where there is obscurity or difficulty, he whispers an explanation in a little unobtrusive note. He hides himself as much as he can; like the prompter on the stage he is never seen, but "gives the word" when wanted. With this we may contrast Dr B. Hill's method, which we find to be neither more nor less than a gigantic system of *note-taking* and extracting from multifarious common-place books—the hunting up of "parallel passages" from other books. Johnson utters an opinion, and something he said elsewhere to the same, or to the contrary effect—or something that some one else has said—is noted, and all these things are "shot" in heaps, and "shovelled" upon the unlucky author, who is himself elbowed quite out of the way.

But the most amazing and distracting of all the editor's inventions is assuredly his system of "parallel passages."

It is difficult to give an idea of the wearisome effect left by these quotations encountered at every page with a monotonous frequency. There is surely a sort of scientific scale in supplying notes. The reader comes on something obscure in the text, and casts his eyes down to the bottom of the page for help, which a mere glance ought to find for him. It is altogether different if he has to encounter a long passage from the *Rambler* or *Spectator*, and which amounts to no more than this, that Johnson had more verbosely expressed the same idea in another place. More tedious still are the laborious references to other portions of the work—the eternal "See *ante*," and "See *post*." The injury thus done to Boswell's sprightly, pleasant chronicle—a light, flowing narrative—were it only in form, is extraordinary. Boswell's own notes are always judicious and artistic—little asides, as it were; an anecdote; a short corrective remark, or gay comment; a short, sufficient sketch of a person alluded to; there are only about half a dozen that seem intruders and too "heavy" for their place. The whole, text and notes, is homogeneous.

After "Walpole's Letters," in nine volumes, his journals, histories, etc., our editor's mainstay for quotation purposes is the *Rambler*, and others of Johnson's works. For every sentiment of Johnson's there is furnished something analogous from his *Rambler*, *Idler*, etc. For this course he gives a singular reason. Johnson, it seems, always talked for argument, so that his conversations could not represent his true opinions. These must be supplied from more orthodox sources. "Editing Boswell," therefore, is to consist in neutralising, correcting, and in part abolishing all these pleasant talks. Cannot our editor understand that the charm of conversation, as of all comedy, is to be found in its spontaneousness and absence of responsibility, and that the speakers are not presumed to "talk upon affidavit," as it were? Their attraction is their being first impressions, and not official utterances, and discursive "laxity of talk" is not to be tested by rule and square.

That this is no exaggerated description of his system is shown by the editor's own testimony. When lying ill in a foreign country, "in the sleepless hours of many a night," he tells us, "I almost forgot my miseries in the delightful pages of Walpole, *and, with pencil in hand, managed to get a few notes taken.*" We may pity as well as admire this honest ardour: but the "getting a few notes taken" from "old Walpole" in the belief that you are "editing" your "Boswell" is but a sad delusion. Again he tells us, "*everything in my reading* that bore on my favourite author was carefully noted," and then—supreme delusion of all!—he fancied that, having gathered a mass of materials "from all sides," they were sufficient to "shield me from a charge of rashness if I began to raise the building"—the "building," by the way, commonly supposed to be Boswell's.

The editor describes how he "discovered Boswell." When he first went to college, "by a happy chance he turned to the study of the literature of the eighteenth century," owing to a sort of theme, set regularly every week, and which consisted in turning into Latin a passage from *The Spectator.* From Addison, in the course of time, he "passed on to the other great writers of his and the succeeding age"; in fact, pursued the ordinary college education. But a solemn moment was at hand. "A happy day came just eighteen years ago, when in an old shop, under the shadow of a great cathedral," our doctor was enabled to secure that uncommon stall-book, "a second-hand copy of a somewhat early edition of the 'Life' in five well-bound volumes." The discovery of this rarity produced quite a revolution. As he made his way through it, astonished and pleased, he began almost unconsciously, as it appeared to him, to edit. And how? "*Before long I began to note the parallel passages and allusions,* not only in their pages, but in the various authors whom I studied. Yet," adds the future editor, naïvely enough, "in these early days I never dreamed of preparing a new edition." And on what trifling things do events turn! Why, who knows that but for that happy day, just eighteen years ago—and that second-hand copy—we might, at this hour, be wandering about without our editor!

The true system of dealing with Boswell's great book goes much deeper than the mere illustrating it with extracts. In one sense it is a great psychological book—a book full of all the various "anfractuosities" of character. It helps us to read off "Jamie's" own nature in a most curious and even piquant fashion. To give one instance. A popular idea is that he was merely the "ambulatory reporter" of the sage's sayings and doings, the exact recorder of his wisdom. But the truth is, that this great "Life" was intended, in a secondary way, as a regular *Apologia* for "Bozzy's" own private failings and weakness, which, as I fancy, he thought he could in some way shelter under the moralities of his great friend. With these he was constantly identifying himself, for he felt the application which his friends would naturally make of Johnson's opinions to his own conduct. The inconsistency of his life and habits with the society and teaching of a great moralist, his constant discussions on religious and moral topics he felt would excite the ridicule of his friends, and this he ingeniously met by the implied confession that he was often but "a weak vessel," but with good purposes and good instincts. He put Johnson forward as making allowance for such failings. This is indeed the general effect left upon the reader, and the result is that Boswell's character comes before us as a very natural and human one. Such an interesting line of enquiry as this would add indeed a fresh piquancy to the study of Boswell, and had been barely hinted at by Mr Croker. Boswell's real purpose was to allot himself a share at least of his great friend's celebrity, and in this he certainly succeeded.

The prosecution of other enquiries of this kind, such as the question of his religion and his religious feeling, and the meaning of his final revolt from Johnson when the latter was on his death-bed, are subjects that take long to investigate, and are not to be despatched as you "go along," or by note-taking.

Next, as to the edition selected by our editor. There are three editions in which Boswell had his share of the preparation from which the editor could make his selection—the first, the second, and the third. The "corrections and additions" made to the second were printed separately in quarto form. Boswell died in 1795, when he was meditating a third edition, and it was not until 1799 that this appeared under the supervision of Edmund Malone; and it is significant of the editorial modesty and reserve in that day, that though he must have expended much labour on his task, his name actually does not appear on the title-page. *O si sic omnes!* In his advertisement he explains in the clearest way what his share in the work was. The corrections given in the second edition had arrived too late to be arranged by the author "in that chronological order which he had endeavoured uniformly to observe," so Boswell had to dispose them "by way of addenda as commodiously as he could." Malone says generally: "In the present edition these additions have been distributed in their proper places," *i.e.* by himself, though in revising the volumes the author had pointed out where "some of these materials" should be placed. Malone then explains that "all the fresh notes that the author had written in the margin of the copy, which he had *in part revised*, are here faithfully preserved." This makes the whole of Boswell's contribution to the new edition. But it would almost seem that he had really only just begun his task, and the reserved phrase, "in part revised," and the notes written on the margin, can hardly be interpreted as meaning more than a few memoranda which Malone naturally made as much of as he could. "A few new notes" were added, principally by friends of the author, and for those without signature "Mr Malone is answerable"—a curious form, considering that the announcement is written by Malone himself.

All these new notes were "enclosed in brackets" to show that they were not written by the author—a piece of respect that might be more imitated. It is evident, indeed, that there was no particular desire that the book should appear to have been edited by anybody. Malone does not claim any share in editing, he merely writes the "advertisement." He even formally disclaims being accountable for typographical errors, as the proofs had not passed through his hands—an unusual thing—the meaning of this being that the family wished that the author should have the full credit of having prepared his own work.

In this state of things it was scarcely worth while for Dr B. Hill to treat it as the third and formal work of the author's. The second was really Boswell's final and most complete effort. But Dr B. Hill tries to justify his preference of this edition by some pleas which seem fallacious enough. He seems to rest his case on these notes which Boswell "wrote in the margin," and which, as I have said, must have been of the fewest and slightest sort. These are not impossible to discover by comparing the two editions. Dr B. Hill, indeed, tells us that he had the whole of the second edition read out to him. "I felt it my duty," he then tells us with solemnity, "to have the whole second edition read aloud to me for comparison with the third," which still would not help him to discriminate between Boswell's and Malone's work; "but, as I read on, *I was convinced* that *about all* the verbal alterations were Boswell's own." This "being convinced" is not much aid. I myself have compared the editions, and can say that there are not half-a-dozen new and additional notes in the whole.

It would be unfair not to allow credit to Dr B. Hill for his unwearied pains and labour, his diligent reading, and the occasionally sagacious "lights" which have cleared away a goodly number of difficulties. I must confess also to feeling some scruple in drawing up this heavy indictment, on account of the genuine enthusiasm and unsparing toil which the editor has brought to his work. But as an unsparing Johnsonian critic himself, he will not be too "thin-skinned." He must recollect, too, the exalted claims that he and his friends have put forward as to the merits of the book, and that there are "Boswellians" as ardent in their faith as he himself, to whom his general treatment of their common idol cannot be acceptable.

DR B. HILL'S "DISCOVERIES."

NATURALLY, having made his first "discovery" of a Boswell in the old shop "under the shadow of a great cathedral," our editor began to find some other wonderful things. Most of these turn out to be either no discoveries at all, or to be all wrong, or made by somebody else. This is generally the case with persons who largely take up a subject of study which delights them; they forget that others have been at work before them, and are too eager and enthusiastic to investigate what these have done.

Lest these "discoveries" of his should be overlooked, the editor makes special mention of them in his preface. We will begin with one notable specimen. Johnson had praised some pretty lines on a girl singing at her wheel, and repeated them: "Verse sweetens toil," etc. Asked where they were to be found, he said he did not recall the name of the poem, but it was by "one Giffard, a parson." The editor went hard to work, and at last discovered the poem. With pardonable pride he claims his meed of praise: "That I have lighted upon the beautiful lines which Johnson quoted, and have found out who 'one Giffard, a parson,' was, *is to me a source of just triumph*. I have not known many happier hours than the one in which, in the library of the British Museum, *my patient investigation was rewarded*, and I perused 'Contemplation.'" Observe what is claimed — patience, long investigation, diligent search, final success and triumph. Willing to sympathise, and wishing to follow in our editor's track, I, at a venture, took down the index to the *Gentleman's Magazine*, Dr B. Hill's old friend, which he has consulted in every difficulty, and was referred to vol. 77, p. 1, page 477, where, to my amazement, I found an account of this "Giffard, a parson," with the passage:—"One small poem of his, entitled 'Contemplation,' was printed in 1752, which attracted the notice of Dr Johnson, who has quoted it in his Dictionary." Bewildered, I next opened another familiar Encyclopædia—Nicholl's "Literary Anecdotes"—and there again was I informed that "Contemplation" was the name of the poem! Next I opened Johnson's great Dictionary. There again it was, under the word "Wheel." The whole process took about five minutes! What did it mean? Where were Dr B. Hill's "patient investigations," "happy hours," and moment of triumph in the Museum? We must not suppose that he would resort to deliberate artifice to enhance his labours; but the incident, at least, calls for some explanation, which Dr B. Hill should consider it due to himself to give.

"I would particularly refer," he says, "to the light I have thrown upon Johnson engaging in politics with Hamilton, and upon Burke's talk of retiring." It is well known that Johnson had formed this connection with Hamilton, and wrote for him a work on "Corn." "But," says the editor, "I suspect there was more than this," as now we shall hear. In the spring of the year 1766, "Burke separated from Hamilton," and it seems to Dr B. Hill "highly probable" that Hamilton then sought Johnson's assistance. In almost the next sentence we are told that Hamilton, "on losing Burke, wrote on February 12, 1765," etc., though we have just been informed that he did not lose Burke until a year later. Then "Chambers was looked for to supply Burke's place," though we have been assured that on "losing Burke" Johnson was applied to. But leaving aside this confusion, we are still uncertain as to "the discovery" made by Dr B. Hill, or "the light" he has "thrown" on the matter. We hear of Warton, Chambers, Burke, Hamilton, but nothing new about Johnson, except an "I think it highly probable."

Next, Dr B. Hill would again particularly refer to "the light I have thrown upon Burke's talk of retiring." Johnson begged him not to think of it, adding that it "would be civil suicide." The editor "discovers" that "the gentleman" was Burke, who had recently said in the House that if a question were pressed he would resign his office. An ordinary reader would see that "retiring" had a more general meaning than this; and indeed it would be absurd to think that a mere resignation would be "*civil* suicide," particularly in the case of such a man as Burke. But the editor should have recalled a passage in "The Tour," under August 19, where Mr Nairne said that he had "an inclination *to retire*," which was regularly discussed by Johnson. He declared that those who were scrupulous "may retire." "I have talked of *retiring*, but I find my *vocation* is an active life." This is conclusive. So much then for the "light thrown" upon Burke's talk of retiring—when it turns out (1) that it was not Burke at all; (2) that he was not "retiring"; and (3) that "retiring" means quite another thing.

There was a page or two which Boswell cancelled in "The Tour," it is supposed under pressure from Sir A. Macdonald, whom he had assailed. The editor assures us that he "discovered, though too late, that in the first edition the leaf containing pp. 167-68 was really cancelled. In my own copy, between pages 168 and 169, there is a narrow projecting ridge of paper," etc.

It may be said that there is no "ridge" between pages 168 and 169; the editor means between pages 166 and 169, but this is a trifle. However this may be, Mr Croker, some sixty years ago, made "the discovery" of the cancel, pasting, ridge, and all! What sort of delusion is this? There is yet another mistake connected with this matter. He tells us that

"Rowlandson, in one of his caricatures, *paints* Boswell as begging for mercy," etc. Now it was not Rowlandson that painted or etched Boswell in such an attitude. The caricature in question belongs to a series of about a score, exhibiting all the most ludicrous incidents of the "Tour," which were the work, as Angelo tells us, not of Rowlandson, but of another artist—one Collins.

Again, he is afraid that ardent advocates of total abstinence will not be pleased at finding that "*I* have been obliged *to show* that Johnson thought that his gout was due to his temperance." To this special attention is called in the preface. To our astonishment, when we come to the body of the work, we find that it was a correspondent of "Notes and Queries," not Dr B. Hill, who found out this opinion of Johnson's!

Yet another of our editor's unlucky guesses is connected with the degree given to Johnson by Oxford. In his Latin reply acknowledging the diploma, he said it had been conferred on him at a time when crafty men were "attempting in every way to impair the fame and influence of the University, attempts which he always had opposed and would oppose." "Here," says the editor, "I believe he alludes to the charge of disloyalty brought against the University." He had in his mind a libellous or disloyal placard which had been posted up in the market-place of the town, and it was reported that this had been done by the students. It was this, according to Dr B. Hill, that was in Johnson's mind. But it will be seen that he talks of "crafty *men*," of attacks which he describes as "storms" (*procellas*). This might dispose of the whole point, but, unfortunately for the editor, Johnson's letter was written in February 1755, and the incident of the placard was in July, five or six months later! So the whole speculation topples over.

This delusion as to sham "discoveries" pursues Dr B. Hill through the whole of his various collections. In the "Letters" there is one for which he is bold enough to claim credit, and which seems really *trop fort.* He must think his readers rather simple folk. On one of his visits to Oxford Johnson had for his host Dr Edwardes, but in his Letters he does not say of what college, or where his rooms were. Now comes forward Dr B. Hill. "In fact, I believe *it is a discovery of mine* that he resided at *Jesus College.*" Wonderful discovery that we can make at once ourselves by turning to any college list! But even granting to him this meagre amount of research, what will be said when we find in one of Hannah More's letters that she was "engaged to dine with *Dr Edwardes of Jesus College*, to meet Dr Johnson"? But let us go on.

The most surprising of Dr B. Hill's "discoveries" I have reserved for the last, and it really takes one's breath away. Goldsmith's age is generally known, or can be known; but our editor has found out that "Goldy" has himself revealed it, or rather hidden it—Donnelly fashion—in a sort of mysterious cryptogram. This is found in his edition of the "Letters": "There is a passage," says the editor, "in *The Bee*, No. 2, which leads me to think that he himself held November twelfth as his birthday. He there says: 'I shall be sixty-two on the twelfth of next November.' Now, as *The Bee* was published in October 1757, he would not be sixty-two, *but just half that number*, *thirty-one*, on his next birthday." This is amazing, and beats the world. A man says he is sixty-two, but means that he is just half that age! But on turning to this *Bee* account, we find not Goldsmith at all, but an account of an elderly gentleman, one "Cousin Jeffrey," in attendance on an old maid, "Cousin Hannah," so that the age of sixty-two was appropriate enough. It is a little tale. And we are called to halve this old gentleman's age to find Goldsmith's! All which seems queer indeed.

So much for the "discoveries," every one of which, it will be noted is a mere dream and delusion.

EXAMINATION OF THE EDITOR'S NOTES, COMMENTS, SPECULATIONS, ETC.

THIS much for the form, arrangement, and discoveries of Dr B. Hill's edition! We shall turn to his profuse notes, which literally whelm and submerge poor Boswell. They are on every conceivable subject, lack relevancy, of course, and in many instances are founded upon a complete misconception of the text. The examination of Dr B. Hill's series of commentaries will, of course, be a long one, but it is well worth making as a "record."

I.

Here is a typical instance: Johnson once suggested to Cave various subjects for essays, such as "Forgotten Poems," or "Loose Pieces like Floyer's," a mere illustration of his suggestion. Boswell does quite enough in supplying this note:—"Sir John Floyer's treatise on the Cold Bath, *Gentleman's Magazine*, 1734, p. 197," his purpose being to mark the subject of one of Johnson's contributions. "But," says the editor, "his letter shows *how uncommon a thing a cold bath was*." Floyer, who, we are assured, recommended "general method of bleeding and purging before the patient uses the cold bath," continues: "I have commonly cured the rickets by dipping children, etc., etc. (For mention of Floyer, see *ante*, etc., and *post*, etc.)." This topic of bathing being started, we go back to Locke, "who in his 'Treatise on Education' recommended cold bathing for children. Johnson, in his review of Lucas's 'Essay on Waters' (*post*, 1756), thus attacks cold bathing," etc. (passage quoted). Then we have Dr Lucas himself: "The old gentleman," he says, "that uses the cold bath," etc.—*Literary Magazine*, p. 229. After which we turn back to the text and find that Johnson was not thinking of any of these things or persons, but had merely suggested the *subject* for a paper!

Johnson once told a good story of a nobleman who wrote a bad play, and then bought up all the copies. At an election, the Duchess of Marlborough had it reprinted with a frontispiece representing an elephant dancing on a tight-rope. All that was wanting was the name of the nobleman—the anecdote, indeed, being suggested to Johnson by the droll rumour that he himself was taking lessons in dancing. Boswell, with his usual restraint, supplies this note. "William, the first Viscount Grimston." Dr B. Hill then starts on his erratic course. "Swift thus introduces him (Lord Grimston)," and Swift's verses are quoted. We next go off to Nichols, who, "in a note on this, says that the author wrote the play when he was a schoolboy." Boswell, observe, was not accountable for this statement, which had nothing to do with Johnson's story; but the editor actively enters into controversy with Nichols on the point. "Two editions were published, *apparently* by Grimston himself, one bearing his name but no date, and the other the date of 1705, but no name. By 1705 he was twenty-two years old—no longer a boy." It might be said that the statement is that the author *wrote* the play when a boy, which is consistent with publishing it when he was grown up. Having done with Nichols, the editor next supplies this extraordinary piece of information: "The former edition *was published by Bernard Lintot* at the Cross Keys, Fleet Street, and the latter *by the same bookseller at the Middle Temple Gate.*" What can this mean? He then proceeds to point a moral: "The grossness of a young man of birth at this period is shown by the preface." No doubt, by "birth," Dr B. Hill means "nobility"; but it happened that the youth was not raised to the peerage until years afterwards. Then we return to further bibliographical details. "*The third edition*, with the elephant, etc., was published in 1736. There is *another illustration* in which an ass is bearing a coronet," etc., and, mark this—"Grimston's name is not given here, but there is a dedication," etc. "Three or four notes are added, one of which is very gross." All which proves that Dr B. Hill is "abroad," as it were, and has little notion of the relevancy of his various odds and ends.

A duel took place between two gentlemen named Riddell and Cunningham, one of whom was killed. Boswell says Cunningham was his "near relation." Our editor makes researches, and finds that "*Boswell's grandfather's grandmother* was a Miss Cunningham; I do not know how it is that this was a near connection." Then follows a jest at the Scotch. "In Scotland, I suppose, so much kindred as this makes two men relatives." But Boswell was not likely to be so absurd, for he says distinctly that the gentleman was his *near* relation; and that he was so nearly connected is evident from the fact that Boswell was sent for by express to his bedside. I find in the pedigrees that Mrs Boswell had a cousin of the name.

When Johnson pleasantly uses a piece of slang "in the phrase of 'Hockley-in-the-Hole,'" the editor gives no less than *sixteen passages* from all sorts and conditions of persons to illustrate the meaning! Johnson had said, jocosely enough, of a little girl: "I being a *buck*, had Miss in to make tea." What need of comment, research, or "editing" here? But Dr B. Hill must discuss the word "Miss." "The word," he says, "at this time was often used in a *loose* sense," and for fear of misapprehension, adds gravely: "Though Johnson could not have so used it." Not likely indeed. Then why introduce the eccentric sense at all? But in proof of his theory he goes on to quote a story from Walpole: how the young Prince Frederick, when Kitty Fisher passed by, being asked, "Who that was?" had answered, "a Miss." Being told that all young ladies were Misses, he said that "she was a particular sort of a Miss that sold oranges." Thus it proved the "loose" sense of the word Miss. The late Peter Cunningham is next called in to prove the fact that orange girls were persons of light character. And all this "skimble-skamble" on Johnson's speech, "I had Miss in to tea"!

"On the 28th of April I went to Bath." Thus wrote Boswell. What *could* be added, unless a full account of Bath, Prince Bladud, Miss Burney, etc.? Dr B. Hill fancies he has "discovered" that all the Abbey bells were set ringing to welcome Boswell, and this purely gratuitous assumption requires forty lines to develop. Goldsmith, it seems, had declared in 1762 that a stranger was always thus welcomed. It does not matter that this was ten years before, and that Boswell himself makes no mention of the salute. "Humphrey Clinker" is then quoted with the same view. But are such speculations "editing"? Boswell next adds: "Mr and Mrs Thrale were gone to the Rooms." This inexpressibly shocks Dr B. Hill, who exclaims: "To the Rooms! and their only son dead three days over one month!" Then a quotation:

> "That it should come to this,
> But two months dead!"—*Hamlet.*

Is it an editor's function to be thus horror-stricken? Nor was it altogether so heinous in the Thrales. "The Rooms" at Bath was the place of common resort—for conversation, for cards, or for music. They were both retired and public. It was natural that the bereaved pair should seek some mild distraction of the kind.

Boswell tells us of one Macbean, who was preparing "a Military Dictionary," and adds in a note: "This book was published." On which our editor: "I have not been able to find it." We are certain that Boswell would not have needlessly obtruded this note if he had not known of or seen the book. I took down Watt's "Bibliotheca," and lo! there I was "able to find it" at once, and in two places!

The following is a fair specimen of the note "brought in by head and shoulders." When Johnson received his degree of M.A., the Chancellor of the University wrote the usual letter of request, signing it "Arran." On which we are told all about the Arrans and the generations of Arrans; how there were three of their family Chancellors, with the history of each. Then we hear of Richardson "writing in 1754 ('Cor.,' ii. 198)," etc.; with a reference to Macaulay ("Essays," iii. 159). Then is introduced a Chancellor, not an Arran at all, "the Earl of Westmoreland, 'old, dull Westmoreland,' as Walpole calls him" ("Letters," i. 290). All this on the bare signature "Arran."

A letter from Johnson, Boswell says, was forwarded from Carlisle to his house at Edinburgh. Our ingenious editor at once introduces Mr Arthur Young ("Tour Through the North of England," iv. 431, 5), "who describes in 1768 some of the roads *along which Boswell* was *to travel nine years later.*" Then follows a long quotation on the "state of the roads," which, after all, might have been improved during the nine years. And all this on a letter addressed to Boswell at Carlisle, sent after him by post! A pleasantly grotesque passage of Boswell's is the little sketch of the "Great Twalmley" and his "New Floodgate Iron," which Boswell explains in a note of about four lines. The Bishop of Killaloe had ironically defended Twalmley as "a benefactor to his species," by applying, in a burlesque way, two lines from Virgil; then the subject dropped. But Dr B. Hill intervenes, and in his own style gravely deals with this trivial matter. In a long note he gives the full passage from Virgil—four lines—with a "translation by Morris," in four lines more. Then, taking up the theme in his own person, he quotes classical passages *in favour* of the great Twalmley, who, he says, "might have justified himself by *The Rambler*, No. 9: 'Every man, from the highest,'" etc. [follows the passage at length]. "*All this is what Twalmley did. He adorned an art*"—*i.e.* invented a sliding-door for a smoothing-iron—"he endeavoured to arrive at eminence, etc. He could also have defended himself by the example of Æneas: *Sum pius Æneas*," etc.

Mr Carlyle, the editor tells us, is in error in describing Johnson as a servitor (on which, it may be said, that "Boswell's Johnson" has no concern with Mr Carlyle's or any one else's misconceptions). "He was a commoner, as the above entry shows"—and Dr B. Hill refers to his own note. One would fancy that it had been uncertain whether Johnson had been a commoner or a servitor, and that Dr B. Hill had "discovered" the fact. But we turn to Boswell's text, and there read, "he was entered as a commoner"!

When M'Leod declared that he would rather drink punch with his tenants than claret in his own house at their expense, he was illustrating the good feeling of Scotch landlords for their dependants. Dr B. Hill gives two passages to prove excessive drinking by *Irish* gentlemen. There is no point or parallel in this. "*Laceration of mind*" Boswell has printed in italics. "*Laceration*," says the editor, "was properly a term of surgery; *hence the italics*." But was not "*of mind*" also in italics? and are those words "terms of surgery" also? This is surely uncritical.

It is often amusing to see how shocked is our editor at certain expressions of his author. As when Gibbon and Langton were elected Professors at the Academy, Boswell said that it reminded him of Swift's "wicked Will Whiston, and good Mr Ditton." There was some pleasantry in this. "But," says our editor gravely, "this poem goes on so grossly and so offensively as regards one and the other, that Boswell's comparison *was a gross insult* to Langton as well as to Gibbon." Boswell was, of course, merely amused at the notion of the oddity of the good man and the heterodox man being chosen together. There are things as offensive in Gulliver, but to compare some one to Gulliver is not an insult. Again: "It is strange"—Dr Hill is always discovering something strange—"that Boswell nowhere quotes the lines in the 'Good-natured Man,' in which Paoli is mentioned." This, as it is so "strange," must have been some compliment, or trait of character, or illustration, but the "lines" in question are simply, "*that's* (a letter) from Paoli of Corsica." Boswell, with his usual acumen, saw that to quote this barren speech contributed nothing to the fame of his hero.

Boswell and his friend were invited to Slains Castle by the Errol family; and the editor shows that it was to Johnson that the invitation was owing, he having been observed in the church by a lady who knew him. On which we have this gloss: "Boswell, *perhaps*, was not unwilling that the reader should think that it was to him that the compliment was paid." Why "perhaps"? No reason is given for this insinuation. But for it there is not a particle of foundation. For he distinctly disclaims all share in the business: "*I had never seen any of the family*, but there had been a card of invitation written by Mr Boyd."

Defending himself from a charge of being a reporter of private conversations, Boswell in a graceful passage asks, "How could any one be annoyed at his not gathering what grew on every hedge?" when "he had collected such fruits as the *Nonpareil* and the *Bon Chretien*." There is a quaint touch here; and by the use of the capitals he seemed to refer to the character of his great friend. But how does it strike our too literal editor? "Both *Nonpareil* and *Bon Chretien are in Johnson's Dictionary. Nonpareil* is defined as a kind of apple, *Bon Chretien* a species of pear." This is literal indeed! Again: in his "Diary" Johnson writes that two sheets of his "Tour" came to him for correction, viz. "F and G." This is plain enough, but our editor must make it plainer still: "F and G are the printer's signatures, by which it appears that at this time sheets *B, C, D, E, had already been printed*."

"I have retained Boswell's spelling" (such as "aweful," etc.), the editor tells us, "for the reason that Boswell, in another work, had said that in case of a reprint he hoped that care would be taken of his orthography." On turning to the work, published twenty-three years before, we find that Boswell was speaking of only *two* forms of spelling, the addition of "k" to "public," and of "u" to such words as "humour," and he trusted that these forms would be adhered to. Dr B. Hill is scarcely justified in forcing or enlarging the meaning in this way.

Dr B. Hill is fond of making out "lists," to wit, "totting up" how many times Johnson was bled, or Boswell was drunk, or how many days the pair were together. It was natural, therefore, when he came to Boswell's proposal to edit Addison's Poems, that it should occur to him to make out a list of all Boswell's projected works. Accordingly, we are told that "he proposed also to publish Johnson's Poems, an account of his own travels, a collection of old Scottish tenures, etc., and a 'History of James IV.'" These items professed to exhaust the matter. But later he begins to mend his hand: "In my list of Boswell's projected works (*ante*, i. 225) I have omitted this, a 'History of Sweden,'" so it now seemed complete. Later again, however, in a note, we are astonished to find the editor taking the subject up once more, and giving us quite a new list. It had now grown to ten items; it looked as though our editor was picking up his information as he went along. However, here at last was a complete final list marked with numerals. But no—turning to the end of the book we find one more new and additional item. And where? Actually put into the index of Boswell's works; "to which must be added 'An Account of a Projected Tour in the Isle of Man'" (where it may be doubted if Boswell *could* have given an account of a tour that was merely "projected," and had not been carried out). Still, we must take our information as we get it, in these "dribs and drabs," as it is called, and rejoice that we have it at last in a complete shape. But what will be said if I can supplement it with some half-a-dozen fresh items which have wholly escaped the editor, and which he is welcome to add to his list in his next edition?

Mistakes of dates occur through the work, such as the statement that Johnson's "Plan of the Dictionary" was published in 1774 (vol. i. p. 176), and that Johnson had been sixteen years in London before he met Hogarth. As their meeting was in 1745-6, and Johnson only came to London in 1737, this cannot be accurate; while the Plan was published over twenty years before the date mentioned.

II.

The note on Johnson's "sliding" is a strange one. Johnson mentions, when he came to college, that on one occasion he was "sliding" on the ice. "Sliding" is an important matter, and needs exhaustive treatment. "This," says our editor, with due gravity, "was on November 6, O.S., *or* November 17, N.S., *a very early time for ice to bear.*" Still there must be *documentary* evidence. "The first mention of frost *that I find in the newspapers of that winter* is in the *Weekly Journal*, where," etc., and a quotation follows. Then is added, "the records of the meteorological observation began a few years later." This "sliding" passage is indeed full of odd things. His tutor Jordan had asked Johnson why he had not attended his lectures, and he answered with much nonchalance "that he had been sliding." This, he explained to Boswell, was "stark insensibility." In another late account he says that he went to his tutor with "a beating heart." Mr Croker thought the two accounts inconsistent; but any one will see that they can be reconciled. Dr B. Hill has what he calls "a very simple explanation." The accounts refer to different hours of the same day: Johnson's "insensibility" belonged to the morning, and his "beating heart" to the afternoon. He had been impertinent before dinner, and when he was sent for after dinner "he expected a sharp rebuke." All of which is rather mythical. There was but the one visit to the tutor, as any one who turns to the passages will see. Johnson *went* to him with a beating heart, dreading punishment, and at the same interview answered him stolidly, from a "stupid insensibility."

Boswell once remarked, "Then Hume is not the worse for Beattie's attack," *i.e.* in his "Essay on Truth." On which the editor introduces an account of a certain picture by Reynolds, in which Beattie is depicted as "the Angel of Truth beating down the vices"; followed by Goldsmith's criticism of the same, at length. Then we are told that one of the figures is said to be a portrait of Hume—a notion which the editor confutes. On his own showing, therefore, there is no *apropos* in introducing the portrait at all. Next, we are oddly told "that Dr Hill Burton *does not mention* the 'Essay on Truth.'" An edition of Boswell could be extended *ad infinitum*, if we set down all the things that modern writers *don't* mention. Next we are assured that "Burns did not hold with Goldsmith, for he took Beattie's side," and a quotation follows.

It is surely needless to repeat in the notes the information given in the text. Boswell in his note speaks of "Dr Douglas, now Bishop of Salisbury"; but the editor in the next column tells us that "Dr Douglas was afterwards Bishop of Salisbury," and, moreover, refers us "*ante*, p. 127," where we find, "Dr Douglas, now Bishop of Salisbury."

"Boswell was no reader," our editor assures us—a rather wholesale assertion. Every critic will have been struck by the extent of Boswell's reading—evidenced not so much by the number of happy quotations from most lánguages as by the tone of general information that pervades his book. But what is the proof offered by the editor? "I wish," wrote Johnson, "you would enable yourself to borrow more;" also Boswell's own confession in 1775, "I have a time of impotency of study" (which many have); and again, "I have promised Dr Johnson to read when I get to Scotland." He had been idle, in fact, and dissipating, and could not then apply to study. But Johnson always gives his friend the highest praise for his reading and knowledge.

The editor, as we have seen, is particularly severe where "morals" or questions of morals arise, and is often shocked at, or reprobates, sentiments or conduct that seem to deviate from his high standard, as in the well-known discussion between Dr Johnson and Lord Auchinleck. The latter, when pressed to name any Scotch religious work of merit, confessed to his son afterwards that he suddenly recollected having seen in a catalogue "Durham on the Galatians," with which he at once "downed" Johnson. There was something pleasant, if not humorous, in this little scene. But the editor deals with it very seriously, and sees here a regular breach of morality. "In the British Museum Catalogue I can find no work by Durham on the Galatians. Lord Auchinleck's triumph was more artful than honest." In other words, he had invented a religious treatise, and thus "lied," as Johnson might say, not only to the sage, but to his own son, to whom he said that he had seen the work. Well, on turning to the British Museum Catalogue, I find "Durham on the Revelations," which the old judge might very naturally have confounded with "the Galatians."

Again, there was an old friend of Johnson's, the well-known Dr James—of powder celebrity

—and for whom he had a cordial affection. The editor, however, has discovered that Johnson "did not speak equally well of Dr James's morals." This is rather a serious charge, for "morals" is a large word. He explains it in this way: "He will not," wrote Johnson, "pay for three box tickets which he took; *'tis a strange fellow.*" Who has not experienced something of this kind—a rich friend forgets to pay, or puts off paying, for some ticket, cab, etc., or is a little stingy—we tell it with a smile—"*'tis a strange fellow*," but we do not thereby revile his "morals." Dr B. Hill has studied books, not character.

Once Johnson, pleased with a dinner, said, "It could not have been better had it been prepared by a 'synod of cooks.'" Could anything be clearer or more intelligible, as a pleasant remark *en passant?* But listen to the editor: "When Johnson spoke of a 'synod of cooks,' *he was, I conjecture, thinking of Milton's 'Synod of Gods,'* in Beelzebub's speech in 'Paradise Lost,' Book II., line 391." It gives one a sort of chill to read these solemnities. But if we must explain it all literally, and "by the card," Johnson was *not* thinking of Milton or Beelzebub, nor even of the Diocesan Synods of his own country; he was drawing a humorous picture of the *chefs* assembled in council, grave as divines, and concocting their dinner.

Boswell described Hawkins as "Mr John Hawkins, an attorney." "In thus styling Hawkins, he remembered, no doubt, Johnson's sarcasm against attorneys." Thus Dr B. Hill: "No doubt." Nothing of the kind. There was no connection between Boswell's speech and Johnson's sarcasm, which was "that he did not like to speak ill of a gentleman behind his back, but he believed he was an attorney." Which prompts Dr B. Hill to engender a new and rather grotesque theory that Johnson "had some motive for his ill-will towards them (the attorneys)," just as he had towards excisemen. And what is the ground for this speculation? That when describing, in his poem, the various bad characters that infested the streets of London, Johnson had used the phrase, "The fell attorney prowls for prey." These are all morbid imaginings. Miss Hawkins expressly states that Boswell used the offensive description of her father because the latter had described him as "Mr James Boswell, a native of Scotland," instead of "the celebrated," or well-known Mr Boswell.

"I mentioned to him," says Boswell, "a respectable person in Scotland whom he knew." Now, who could see any obscurity here? But we have a long disquisition on the meaning of the word "respectable." In those days "it was *still* a term of high praise." The dictum, as it is needless, we might let pass. But it must be proved by quotations, firstly from Johnson's Dictionary; secondly, from "The Tour"; thirdly, from Dr Franklin; fourthly, from the *Gentleman's Magazine;* fifthly, from Hannah More; sixthly, from Gibbon; seventhly, from George III.; eighthly, from Lord Chesterfield! All these personages, it seems, used "respectable" as "a term of praise."

When Mrs Thrale contemptuously described Boswell as "sitting steadily down at the other end of the room" to take notes of the conversation, the editor suggests that "stealthily" should be read. But Mrs Thrale meant that Boswell pursued his work with a sort of obtuse purpose or "doggedness," regardless of remark. He never had any idea of "stealthiness" in his task. The Prince of Wales had promised to attend the Royal Academy Exhibition, and Johnson wrote that "when we had waited an hour and a half he sent us word that he could not come." This quite puts the editor in a rage. "The First

Gentleman of Europe was twenty-one years old when he treated men like Johnson and Reynolds with this insolence." From this rhapsody one would fancy it was the banquet or a deputation when a number of important people, such as Johnson and Reynolds, were kept waiting. Johnson meant that they were expecting the Prince for an hour and a half, it being the opening of the Exhibition, which was attended by hundreds. There was no "insolence" in this; he was so far polite that he sent his excuses; neither had the Prince at that time any claim to be "First Gentleman in Europe." And, finally, the anecdote is not in Boswell.

Sometimes our editor indulges in a joke. On the mention of "Jackson the all-knowing," we have this most singular note: "Mr Croker gives a reference to p. 136 of his edition. Turning to it, we find an account of Johnson, who rode upon three horses. It would seem from this that because John = Jack, therefore Johnson = Jackson." This tone of treating Boswell's great book is surely indecorous. No one of true editorial tact would indulge in such a remark. Besides, it is merely a slip of the index matter, and there are many as bad in the editor's own index. It was, further, a not unnatural mistake, the eyes being deceived by the likeness of the two names.

Boswell speaks of one of Hogarth's prints which, with others, "was pasted on the walls of the dining-room at Streatham." This trifling matter seems clear enough, save to Dr B. Hill. He wonders "whether pasted is *strictly used*," and thinks it likely "that a wealthy brewer would have afforded Hogarth a frame." He cannot see that it was no question of saving or "affording," but of decoration; this pasting of prints on screens and walls has often been seen in old houses. What, too, is the "strict use" of the word "pasted"? No one could speak of a frame being "pasted" to a wall, even in the less strict use of "pasted." At any rate, Boswell had seen the pictures, and says they were "pasted."

III.

Here is an odd delusion of our editor's. He conceived a theory that Boswell "looked down" on Mr Thrale as being a person in trade, because he spoke of him as "Thrale," not as Mr Thrale; and of his house as "Thrale's." Why, in the very two pages that Dr B. Hill points to, we find Boswell speaking of his friend as "*Mr* Thrale" no less than *eleven times!* The theory is wholly fanciful. Again, the editor, announcing a future collection of Johnson's letters, to be edited by himself, sets out this remarkable doctrine: "While the correspondence of David Garrick has been given to the world in *two large volumes, it is not right* that the letters of his far greater friend should be left scattered and almost neglected." Apart from this odd *non sequitur* and the appeal to comparative *size*, the editor's argument is based on a mistake. Johnson's letters are not "left scattered." All that is valuable is found in Boswell's work, and in Mrs Piozzi's volumes. Neither can they be called "neglected," or at least more neglected than they would be in the new shape proposed. But, again, in spite of the "two large volumes," Garrick's letters are still "left scattered." There are many in MS., many in the *Monthly Mirror*, *European*, and *Gentleman's Magazines*. Again, more than one-half of the two large volumes are other persons' letters. So in every view Dr B. Hill is unlucky.

And again, when Boswell objected to keeping company with a notorious infidel, "a celebrated friend of ours" said to him, "I do not think that men *who live laxly in the world, as you and I do*, can with propriety assume, etc. It is not consistent to shun an infidel to-day and *get drunk to-morrow.*" Dr B. Hill actually debates the point that Burke could not be the person who lived laxly! For Burke was always "eminent friend." "Moreover," he adds, with perfect gravity, "Burke *was not in the habit of getting drunk.*" Nor did he "live laxly in the world." Then Dr B. Hill thinks of Hamilton, a most sober, respectable personage, and whom Boswell also spoke of as "celebrated," and whom nobody thought lived laxly, etc. But then Boswell and Hamilton were not "friends." Had the editor reflected a little he would have found the person that suited exactly—Windham, who both lived laxly and got drunk.

Boswell, speaking of Harry Dundas, had alluded to his strong Scotch accent, and the editor says: "There is no doubt malice in this second mention of Dundas's accent." As a ground for this malice, he instances Boswell's complaints of neglect. But let us see what is this "malicious" passage: "I cannot too highly praise Mr Dundas's speech. His Scottish accent has often been obtruded as an objection to his powerful abilities," etc. He then likens him to the "most eminent orators of antiquity," in fact, indulges in extravagant panegyric. The truth was, the prudent Boswell was complimenting Dundas in the hope of obtaining his patronage.

Johnson wrote to his black servant exhorting him to be "a good boy." The editor enters on a serious calculation of years, and actually proves by dates that he was not "a boy"! Of course the reader sees that Johnson was using a familiar colloquial phrase. "Be a good boy and take care of yourself," is the refrain of a ballad. In other instances he tries hard to prove that women were not to be called "girls."

"A gentleman," says Boswell, "supposed a case," etc. "The gentleman," the editor says, "must have been Boswell himself, for no one else was present." But Boswell was too careful a workman to overlook this. On turning to the passage, it will be seen that it was a reminiscence, Boswell suspending his account of the conversation to introduce it. For he says: "And let it be kept in mind that he was very careful not to encourage," etc., giving as an illustration, "A gentleman supposed a case." And, on resuming, he is careful to say: "He, *this evening*, expressed himself," etc.

Some of the editor's "illustrations" only illustrate the contrary sense of the passage—as when Johnson declared that "hardly any one died without affectation." We have Madame de Sevigné to the effect that there is often long acting of a comedy during life, "but that at death we tell the truth"; and also Young, who speaks of "dropping the mask" at death.

"Boswell liked to display such classical learning as he had." Thus the editor, generalising. But it turns out that he was dining with the Headmaster of Eton, and frankly confessed that, to keep up his credit in such company, he furbished up some quotations, which was most natural, "talking," in fact, "ostentatiously." And on this is founded a *general* statement.

At a dinner, when "The Dunciad" came under discussion, "one of the company," says Boswell, having remarked, "And a poem on what—on dunces?" Johnson rudely attacked him. "Ah, it was worth while being a dunce then! Hadst *thou* been living," etc. The editor thinks that this "one of the company" was Boswell. The dinner was in 1769, in the early stages of Boswell's intimacy with the sage, and long before he had begun to make rude speeches to him. The dinner was given *by* Boswell—he was the host—neither was he in anything approaching to a dunce. There was one present, however, who was a favourite butt of Johnson, and of whom he was always speaking contemptuously—Tom Davies—and *he* was certainly the man.

"A ghastly smile" is a common expression enough; but we are informed that it is "borrowed from 'Paradise Lost,' II., 846."

Speaking of Miss Knowles's "sutile" pictures or embroidery, Johnson said, "Staffordshire is the nursery of art; here they grow up till they are transplanted to London." Who would suppose that he was thinking of anything but of the local artists? No. "He is pleasantly alluding to the fact that he was a Staffordshire man." How "pleasantly"? and what had Johnson to do with "art"? and where is the "allusion"?

When the travellers were at Inverness, a clergyman who preached spoke of persons who connected themselves with men of talent, and tried to deck themselves with their merits. Boswell naïvely says that "he thought this was an odd coincidence." But Dr B. Hill sees no coincidence, and finds it "odd that Boswell did not suspect the parson," who had no doubt learnt that they were to be present at his sermon. Could any one of critical taste believe that a clergyman, in his church, could adopt this offensive mode of "preaching at" two strangers? And if he *did* know of their presence, the obscure clergyman of a remote Scottish district could never have heard of the town jests on Boswell's attendance on Johnson. He would, if anything, have been complimentary and full of respect, but, it is likely, did not know till later that he had the great Dr Johnson and his friend listening to him. Boswell, speaking of Lord Monboddo's ill-feeling to Johnson, said that the latter was "even kindly, as appeared from his enquiring of me after him by an abbreviation of his name. 'Well, how does Monny?'" But our editor looks grave. There is more underneath. "The use," says the editor, "of the abbreviation *Monny* on Johnson's part *scarcely seems a proof of kindness.*" Yet pet names usually betoken good humour and affection. More odd are the instances by which he supports his theory. Johnson had said that on several occasions "Sherry was dull"; "Mund Burke" was "lacking in sense"; and "Derry" (Derrick) had "outrun his character." Here were proofs of "unkindness." Any one that turns to the passages will see that Johnson was, as it were, affectionately lamenting certain little weaknesses in friends he loved. At the worst, no one could contend, as the editor actually seems to do, that the *use* of a pet name was a proof of unkindness.

Johnson spoke of its being said that Addison wrote some of his best papers "when warm with wine." A note of sixteen lines is furnished, giving an account of how Addison spent his day, finishing it at a tavern, where "he often drank too much wine." This, it will be seen, does not prove or illustrate the statement that he *wrote* when warm with wine. Boswell adds that Blackstone wrote his commentaries with a bottle of port before him, on which is a most extraordinary, heterogeneous note of thirty lines. It opens with a quotation from Mr Foss, proving that the judge did *not* take exercise, that he was corpulent, etc. "*His portrait in the Bodleian shows that he was a very fat man.*" Then Scott "would not have thought any the worse of Blackstone for his bottle of port"; and we are told he and his brother, Lord Eldon, relished port wine, the fact being it was one of the favourite drinks of the time. Then "some one asked him whether Lord Stowell took much exercise," etc. "Yet both men got through a vast deal," etc. These undiscriminating odds and ends are bewildering. How much more interesting it had been if Dr B. Hill had studied his text on true editorial principles. This passage he would have found gave some displeasure to the Blackstone family. Boswell altered it, adding a compliment, "and found his intellect invigorated," etc. This is more to the point than being told that "he was a very fat man."

Johnson had found fault with the meat in Paris. The editor, to confute him, quotes Smollett, who found it "extremely good." But this was twelve years before Johnson's visit. We next have Walpole, who complained of the want of "clean victuals, good tea, butter," etc. But this was at *Amiens*, not at Paris, and Walpole does not mention *meat* at all. Finally, there is Goldsmith, who indeed speaks of the "tough meat" at Paris. So Johnson is right after all.

Speaking of Lord Hailes, formerly Sir David Dalrymple, the editor needlessly cautions us that "he is not to be confounded with *Sir John* Dalrymple." We might as well be warned not to confound Mr W. H. Smith with Mr Samuel Smith, or Mr John Morley with Mr Samuel Morley, or Sir John Sullivan with Sir Arthur Sullivan. "Boswell nowhere quotes Mrs Barbauld's fine lines on 'Corsica.'" Why should he? There is an abundance of verses, essays, etc., on the subject which he does *not* quote. He was writing Johnson's life. So odd does this abstinence appear to the editor, that he devises this odd theory to account for it. "He must have been ashamed to quote the praise of the wife of one described by his great friend as 'a little Presbyterian schoolmaster.'" Johnson said jocosely that Beattie "had *sunk upon them* that he had a wife." This is quite intelligible. Beattie himself said that he understood it as "studiously concealing." What need of more? Still the editor must apply to the great Dictionary, where, he says reprovingly, Beattie "would have found this explanation: 'To suppress: to conceal.'" But this *was* Beattie's meaning. Then Dr B. Hill quotes Swift's advice to servants, where he tells them, if sent to buy an article, they were to "sink the money," which is not Johnson's meaning, but a new one, "to appropriate."

IV.

One of the editor's speculations is rather confused and uncritical, as the reader will judge. "I cannot but wish," says Boswell, speaking of the *Rambler*, "that he had not ended it with an unnecessary Greek verse;" and he adds: "How much better would it have been to have ended it with a prose sentence," etc. Here the editor exclaims: "I have little doubt that this *attack* is an indirect blow at Hawkins, who had quoted the whole passage, and had clearly thought it more 'aweful' on account of the couplet." Without going further, every reader feels that this is quite a delusion, and that Boswell was not thinking of such a trifle. He always names Hawkins when he attacks him. But there was no "attack," and on turning to Hawkins, we find not the slightest allusion to the couplet, or that he "clearly thought" the passage "more awful" because of it. He limits his praise wholly to the *prose* paragraph, which he calls awful. What Dr B. Hill was thinking of when he engendered this theory I cannot imagine. Finding an allusion to the death of two booksellers, he turns to his *Gentleman's Magazine* to find their names—"Mr Paul Knapton and Thomas Longman, Esq."—on which he calls attention to the high relative position of the Longmans above their fellows, even thus early; poor Knapton being only plain "Mr," the other being garnished with "Esq." The truth is, Knapton stood far higher, being an old-established bookseller, whose name is on innumerable title-pages; and the obituary notes in the *Gentleman's Magazine* were copied from the newspapers, where they were inserted by relatives with "Esq." if they preferred it.

Lord Campbell stated that Hunter, Johnson's

master, was celebrated for having flogged seven boys who all became judges. "Here," the editor says, "he blunders," *because* Northington and Clarke were from Westminster School. This does not prove the blunder, for Wilmot, one of the seven, after being under Hunter, also went to Westminster School, as the others might have done, Hunter's being merely a country Grammar School.

Johnson had written to his printer: "I will take the trouble of altering any stroke of satire which you may dislike," and Boswell naturally praises him for his "humility in allowing the printer" to alter what he disliked. But the editor tells us that Boswell "*misread* the letter"; he did not offer to allow the printer to make alterations! Surely this is a poor quibble. The printer was to point out the alteration he required, and that was making an alteration.

Boswell repeats the well-known saying of Goldsmith, as to Malagrida and Lord Shelburne, adding a short defence of his friend. All that was necessary by way of note might be a line on Malagrida. But Dr B. Hill gives quotations from Voltaire, Wraxall, and his favourite "Fitzmaurice's Shelburne": "Anybody who examines Reynolds' picture of Shelburne, *especially about the eyebrows*," etc. Then we learn that "Beauclerk wrote to Lord Charlemont," etc., and the whole Goldsmith story is given over again, in the midst of which the editor interpolates this sentence: "Shelburne supported Townshend in opposition to Wilkes in the election of Lord Mayor. ('Fitzmaurice's Shelburne,' II. 28.)" So Goldsmith makes a blundering speech, and away we travel in pursuit of Malagrida, Shelburne and his eyebrows, Charlemont, Beauclerk, Lord Mayors, Townshend, Wilkes.

Johnson was assailing the ignorance and idleness of the Scotch clergy. To illustrate this, Dr B. Hill quotes a long description of certain clergymen and their roysterings, given by Dr Carlyle. We find that these were *English* clergymen, and that the scene was at Harrogate!

The editor often gives us notes upon his own notes. Thus when Johnson advocated the procession of malefactors to Tyburn, we have no less than *sixty* lines from Richardson, describing the ceremonial. In this Richardson passage unluckily occurs the mention of a particular psalm sung on the occasion, which then embarks us on a new quotation from Pope to prove that it *was* the custom for such a psalm to be sung. Boswell and his friend then discussing some recent executions—which, from their number, were certainly barbarous enough—our editor conjures up this fanciful picture of Johnson: "There is something dreadful in the thought of the old man quietly going on with his daily life within a few hundred yards of this shocking scene of slaughter." Why "dreadful"? The thought never occurred to him. Nay, he was for a public procession of the criminals, which he thought was for the general good. Or, supposing that it so affected him, why should he not "go on with his daily life"? Dr B. Hill's idea of distance, too, is as fanciful as his speculation. Bolt Court was nearly half a mile from Newgate—many streets and many blocks of buildings interposed, notably the great Fleet Prison. The scene was in another district altogether.

Johnson's speech to Windham on going to Ireland is well known: "Don't be afraid, sir; you will soon make a very pretty rascal." The editor's odd comment is: "The Whigs thought he made a very pretty rascal in a different way;" in proof of which he tells us that Romilly was "astonished" at his opposing a School Bill and the repeal of an Act of Parliament. This is as extraordinary as it is perplexing. Johnson had advised him to claim everything—to use all arts for getting on: "Don't be afraid, sir; you will soon make a pretty rascal." And this the editor thinks is the same thing as opposing two Whig measures: and he gratuitously asserts that the Whigs thought Windham a very pretty rascal for doing so.

Here is a very serious misapprehension of the meaning. The editor, after mentioning that Johnson would not attend the Presbyterian worship in Scotland, points out his inconsistency, for "in France he went to a Roman Catholic service." On turning to the passage, we find that he happened to enter St Eustache when the children were being catechised, and listened to the curé's instruction, which was not "a service" at all. These exaggerations are constantly met with. Boswell once fondly reminded Johnson how they first conceived the plan of their "Tour" at the Mitre Tavern. The editor corrects him: "It was at the Turk's Head Coffee-House." On turning to the passage referred to by the editor in proof, we find Boswell merely saying that "We talked of the plan at the Turk's Head"—without a word of its being the *first* time. Boswell distinctly says it was at the Mitre.

On the journey to Harwich, Johnson and Boswell stopped the night at Colchester. The editor is sorely puzzled. "They left London early, and yet they only travelled fifty-one miles that day;" twenty more miles, and they would have been at Harwich. But he might have learned the explanation from Boswell himself. They wished to see the town, which Johnson "regarded with veneration as having stood a siege for Charles I."; and the friends wished to be together for another day.

Dr B. Hill has a curious morbid delusion as to what is "indecent," and flings about imputations of this kind. Against the worthy Cave he brings this charge, accusing him of inserting in his magazine "verses as gross as they are dull," advertisements of "indecent books," one of which is "in very gross language." I have not been able to search out these specimens; but we may test the editor's statement by his charge against Johnson of accepting an "Epilogue" for his "Irene," which is a "little coarse and a little profane." In this, jocose allusion is made to the Turkish system of a husband "with fifty wives," and the speaker says she prefers the English system of one husband to herself, instead of having a fiftieth part of one. I cannot see any "coarseness" in this "Epilogue." The "profanity" may be searched for in vain, unless the editor means that the word "devil" is profane.

When Mrs Johnson died, the editor notes that her name did not appear in the usual monthly list of deaths in the *Gentleman's Magazine*. "Johnson," he adds rather bitterly, "did not, I suppose, rank among eminent persons." Now, Johnson was not, at the time, an eminent person. He had not published his Dictionary. Mrs Johnson, at least, was not an "eminent" person; and, finally, the list was not one of eminent persons at all.

"Frank," Johnson's servant, had entered the Navy, and Johnson indirectly sought Wilkes's aid to obtain his discharge. The application to Wilkes was on March 20; and the editor speculates: "Had he been discharged at once, he would have found Johnson moving from Gough Square to Staple Inn," which removal took place on March 25. There is no ground for presuming that he would have been discharged on this particular day, even if he had been discharged "at once." The letter had to reach Wilkes, who had to apply: the matter had then to be considered; so it would have taken months. But that the speculation is wholly idle is proved by what Boswell tells us, that the man "*was at sea*," probably at some far-off station. Finally, it took over a year to obtain the discharge.

Johnson spoke of the little use there was found in Lectures; on which the editor suggests that "perhaps Gibbon had seen this passage when he wrote something of the kind in his 'Memoirs.'" Perhaps *not*. Gibbon wrote his "Memoirs" in 1789, and the passage alluded to is found near the opening. Boswell's work appeared two years later; so Gibbon could not have seen it when he wrote. And how uncritical to suppose that a Gibbon would *borrow* from a Boswell.

And a singular, unaccountable speculation is that of the editor's on Gibbon's change of religion at Oxford, of which Boswell and Johnson spoke rather contemptuously. Gibbon says, in his "Memoirs," that "many years afterwards this report was industriously whispered at Oxford." The editor actually asks us to believe that this large statement refers, "I have no doubt, to the attacks made on him" here by Boswell and Johnson! Gibbon left Oxford in 1753, and the attack was in 1776. The report, "industriously circulated at Oxford," applied to the community *there;* not to the two friends, who had picked it up because it was "industriously circulated." There is the difficulty that Gibbon's "Memoirs" end with the year 1788, three years before the appearance of Boswell's "Life"; so the editor engenders a theory that "he wrote a portion of them, *I believe*, after the publication of the 'Life.'" This, "I believe," will hardly do.

V.

I could give dozens of instances where Dr B. Hill completely misapprehends his text. Thus, Johnson condemned petitions "as a new mode of distressing the Government and its measures." "*Yet*" — wishing to show how inconsistent Johnson is — "yet he was angry when Dr Dodd's petition was neglected, and the public called for mercy." In this case he was speaking of a petition to the *King*, who was the only fountain of mercy: in the other case he was alluding to those who distressed the *Government*—quite different things.

When Mrs Knowles, the Quakeress, spoke of "the bright regions where pride and prejudice can never enter," the editor asks, "Did Miss Austen find here the title of 'Pride and Prejudice' for her novel?" Mrs Knowles was arguing against the pride and prejudice which Johnson displayed; the passage is found, too, not in Boswell, but in the *Gentleman's Magazine*, which Miss Austen was not likely to have consulted for her titles.

The editor seems always to have had Johnson's great Folio Dictionary beside him, which he consulted on meeting any unusual word. A favourite form with him is, "*This word is not in Johnson's Dictionary*," which is about as valuable as the statement that "Crummles is *not* a Prussian." We are told this again and again. Mr Dempster, writing in praise of Johnson's "Tour," used the word "fossilist," when we are assured that "this word is not found in Johnson's Dictionary." The editor must be reminded, firstly, that it was a point of no importance what words Dempster used, or whether they were in or out of Johnson's Dictionary; secondly, that the Dictionary did not include all words in use; thirdly, that numbers of words had come into use since the Dictionary was published; and, finally, that the point is utterly trivial, and not worth noticing.

Johnson, in delight at his return to Oxford, wrote: "* * * is now making tea." "Perhaps Van," says the editor, "for Vansittart." This gentleman is named in the next sentence of the text as the person to whom Johnson suggested "climbing over a wall." Then, why should his name be suppressed in the matter of making tea? The three stars more probably stand for some lady's name. But this is a trifle. Johnson then tells of his delight at being back at his old University—how he was never out of his gown, had "swum," had proposed climbing the wall—a rather touching state of exultation. But our editor thinks that he had taken too much wine! "Johnson *perhaps* proposed climbing over the wall on the day on which University College witnessed his drinking three bottles of port." This might have been in some "gaudy" during his undergraduate course; there is no evidence that it was during this visit.

"I remember," says Johnson, "when people changed a shirt only once a week." As was to be expected, we have a dissertation on shirt-changing, going back to the *Tatler*, where it is mentioned that a shirt was changed twice a week. Gay, by selling stock, might have had a clean shirt every day. Then we have Tristram Shandy, the Spiritual Quixote, and Mrs Piozzi, all brought in.

"Foote," the editor tells us, "had taken off Lord Chesterfield in the 'Cozeners.'" Foote had "taken off" many persons, that is, had brought them on the stage, mimicked their dress, peculiarities, speech, etc. Dr B. Hill then gives as a specimen Mrs Aircastle's speech: "I wish you would read some late posthumous letters; you would know the true value of the graces." This is not "taking off" Lord Chesterfield.

Johnson laid it down that "the public practice of any art," such as portrait-painting, was "improper in a woman"; for, "staring at men's faces was indelicate." Here the editor tries to convict him of inconsistency: "Yet he sat to Miss Reynolds perhaps ten times." Johnson was speaking of the "*public*" practice, that is, of *professional* portrait-painting—the "staring" at *strange* men. *He* was not a strange man.

VI.

Here is another of the editor's odd dreams. "Dryden, Pope, Reynolds, Northcote, Ruskin, *so runs the chain of genius*, with only one weak link in it." This seems mysterious and queer, to say nothing of the "chain running," but it is thus explained. When Reynolds was in the country, Northcote succeeded in touching his coat. "In like manner, Reynolds had touched the hand of Pope." Pope persuaded some one "*to take him to a coffee-house* which Dryden frequented." This was not much. "*Who*," exclaims Dr B. Hill, "*touched old Northcote's hand?* Has the Apostolic succession been continued?" But he can tell us: "I have read with pleasure" that Mr Ruskin was taken to have his portrait done by "old Northcote." No "touching" here; so there are two "weak links" in the chain. We could make a chain "run" in better fashion, which has at least some connection with Johnson. Persons now alive have "touched" Mr Croker; Mr Croker touched Lord Stowell; Lord Stowell, Johnson; Johnson, George III., and so on. And all this on the text that Johnson and Reynolds travelled in Devonshire.

"Boswell, according to the Bodleian Catalogue, was the author of 'Dorando.'" But is this all Dr B. Hill can tell us on this interesting point? The cataloguer's authority is of no moment. I have investigated the matter, and, if the editor turn to my "Life of Boswell," it can be shown clearly that Boswell was the author.

"Johnson had offended Langton, as well as Goldsmith, this day, yet of Goldsmith only did he ask pardon. Perhaps this increased Langton's resentment." Let us compare the two cases. To Langton he had said, "I wonder how a gentleman of your piety can introduce such a subject." And Langton humbly replied he only did so to learn Johnson's views. But to Goldsmith, Johnson had said, outrageously enough, "*Sir, you are impertinent.*" In the first case no apology was needed—in the other it was given. Johnson furnished Goldsmith with a few lines for "The Traveller"; on which the editor: "For each line of 'The Traveller' Goldsmith was paid 11¼d. *Johnson's present, therefore, of nine lines was, if reckoned in money, worth* 8s. 5¼d." Is there not something rather *mesquin* in this sort of criticism? Neither was Goldsmith paid by the line, but received a sum for the whole. Had Johnson not contributed, he would have received the same sum. In the same spirit we are told that when "Johnson this year accepted a guinea from Robert Dodsley, for writing an introduction, *he was paid at the rate of little over twopence a line.*"

When Foote supplied beer to a house the servants refused to drink it; but a black who heard his jests at dinner, was so delighted that he declared in the kitchen he *would* drink his beer. Somebody then remarked that Garrick would not have produced this effect, and Wilkes said "that he would have made the beer still smaller. He will play 'Scrub' all his life." Dr B. Hill here strangely fancies that there is an allusion to a speech of Scrub's: "On Saturday I draw warrants and on Sunday I *draw beer.*" Wilkes meant that Garrick was like Scrub in his mean ways.

"A fig for my father (Boswell's) and his new wife." Thus Johnson. "It is odd," the editor thinks, "that, as Lord Auchinleck had been married more than six years, his wife should be called new." There is nothing odd; for later, Johnson talks of Boswell's "new mother." She was new compared with the old wife of thirty years' standing.

One of the signers of the famous "Round Robin" was a certain "Thos. Franklin" (without the "c"), about whom the editor can discover nothing. He is certain, however, that it was *not* a well-known Professor Dr Thos. Francklin, (with a "c"). The reader shall judge. This gentleman was a dramatist, the intimate friend of Garrick, Johnson, and Goldsmith. The "Round Robin" was signed at a dinner at Reynolds' house. Francklin was his intimate friend also, and, moreover, Professor at the academy whereof Reynolds was President. Can there be a doubt as to the man? As to the "c," says the editor, "The Rev. Dr Luard has kindly compared six signatures of Francklin, ranging from 1739 to 1770, which all have the 'c.'" But this "Round Robin" dinner was in 1776, six years later. In one of his notes on the careless spelling of names at this era, the editor admits that "Johnson spelt Boswell with one 'l,'" etc.

Johnson had said, "Nobody attempts to dispute that two and two makes four." "Nobody, that is to say, but Johnson," adds the editor. For proof of this charge we are referred to Dr Burney: "If you said two and two make four, he would say, 'How do you prove that?'" But Dr Burney was speaking of Johnson's not allowing people to make idle "assertions," on which he would call for proof. Further, it was not Johnson who disputed that two and two made four, but Burney, who *supposed* the case of his doing so! And, even under the supposition itself, he never disputed the fact. But what settles the matter is, that Johnson in one place says, "You may have a reason why two and two make five, but they will still make but four."

"A gentleman" attacked Garrick for being vain. "Very likely Boswell," explains the editor, bidding us "See *post*" in proof, where we find that Boswell "slyly introduced Mr Garrick's name, and his assuming the airs of a great man."

But why would Boswell *conceal* his own name in the one passage, and reveal it in the other? Further, to "attack" Garrick was not Boswell's way. And still further, in this second passage, he actually *joins* in Garrick's praises. It is obvious that "the gentleman" was *not* Boswell.

Here is a curious instance of a misunderstanding of a passage. Johnson wrote to Lord Elibank that he never met him without going away a wiser man. "*Yet*," objects the editor, "he said of him there is nothing *conclusive* in his talk." But the two things are compatible. Johnson, on this last occasion, was praising Oglethorpe's "variety of knowledge," though he owned he was desultory and "never completed what he had to say." On which Boswell, "He, *on the same account*, made *a similar* remark on Lord Elibank. 'Sir, there is nothing *conclusive*,'" etc.; *i.e.* he does not complete, etc. But his talk was wise. Nothing could be clearer.

Boswell was speaking of Goldsmith's "envy" of people who were "distinguished," and which he exhibited to a ridiculous extent. The editor quotes a person to whom the poet said that "he himself *envied* Shakespeare." This is not the sort of envy Boswell means. Johnson declared that inoculation had destroyed more lives than war. The editor, wishing to prove this wholesale statement, quotes a longish account of Dr Warton, whose daughter was inoculated, and died!

Johnson, when on his deathbed, directed a stone to be placed over the grave of his father and mother in a Lichfield church. It has, however, disappeared. It is obvious that the point of the incident is Johnson's filial affection; but it leads the editor into the most rambling speculations about the "stone." Why was it not there? What became of it? Was it ever there? In his distress he calls for the aid of the Rev. James Serjeatson, the rector, who, from his office, is assumed to have special knowledge, though he can have known little of the matter; but the rev. gentleman is even more wild in his speculations. "He suggests to me that the stone was never set up" (*query*, set down?) for the reason that "it was unlikely that within a dozen years such a memorial was treated so unworthily." In vain the worthy historian of the town, Dr Harwood, who must have seen "the stone," distinctly records that it was taken away in 1796, when the church was paved—a common incident. But this will not do. The "stone" was never placed there; for "there may have been some difficulty in finding the exact place of the interment." All which is a gratuitous fancy; for Johnson particularly directed that the spot was to be found, before ordering the stone; and we are told that the mason's receipt "shows that he was paid for the stone." Then we have this odd theory: "The matter may have stood over till it was forgotten;" and, last and wildest hypothesis of all, "the mason may have used it for some other purpose." This in the face of the facts that the stone was ordered, laid, and removed!

Johnson once wished "he had learned to play at cards." "*On the other hand*," begins Dr Hill, "he says in his *Rambler* that a man may shuffle cards, or play at dice from noon till midnight, and get no new idea." Cannot Dr B. Hill see that he is here speaking of gambling, as his allusion in the same paper to "agitated passions and clamorous altercations" clearly shows?—another thing altogether from learning to play whist.

Johnson spoke of the respect shown to officers, and how they were everywhere well received. But, says Dr B. Hill, "in his thoughts on the coronation he expressed himself differently;" and adds, "if, indeed, the passage is of his writing." But there all he says is that "it offends us to see soldiers placed *between a* man and his sovereign"—that is, he objected to the system of body-guards! So he did not "express himself differently." Johnson having added that when a common soldier was civil in his billet or "quarters," he was treated with respect, we are given a long note on the Mutiny Act, the amount of food to be furnished, what the innkeepers had to supply—lodging, fire, candlelight, five pints of beer per diem, etc. All this on the mention of the single word "quarters."

Sheridan's wife, we are told, had £3000 settled on her, "with delicate generosity," by a person to whom she had been engaged, and for which Dr B. Hill quotes Moore. He apparently does not know that this sum was forced from the gentleman as damages for a breach of contract. He really behaved atrociously to the lady, and was gibbeted by Foote in "The Maid of Bath"; so he displayed no "delicate generosity" at all.

Johnson protested that he would not keep company with a fellow "whom you must make drunk before you can get the truth from him." Dr B. Hill supplies a note from Addison which has no bearing on the matter: "Our bottle conversation is infected with lying." One would think that this is general, and shows that wine breeds untruthfulness; but on turning to the passage we find Addison deploring the general reign of lying—in society and everywhere; "even our bottle conversation," he adds, "is infected," etc. And, observe, Johnson was thinking of drunkenness, and Addison of drinking merely—different things.

A remark was made that in the northern parts of Scotland there was very little light in winter. "Then," writes Boswell, "we talked of Tacitus." Here Dr B. Hill speculates, and ventures to fill up "out of his own head" all that occurred between the two subjects. "Tacitus, 'Agricola,' chapter xii., was, no doubt, quoted in reference to the shortness of the northern winter's day." But in such a case Boswell would have been only too glad to add something dramatic to his narrative by giving the steps of the transition. "My revered friend then said, 'It is extraordinary, Sir, how the ancients anticipated these things. Tacitus, in his "Agricola,"'" etc. But Boswell, as he does in so many places, passed to, or "introduced" a new subject, perhaps a little abruptly.

Boswell speaks of "Mr Orme, the able historian" of India. As an illustration, the editor tells of Colonel Newcome, whose "favourite book was a History of India—the history of Orme." What is the value of that? On this principle, if Gibbon be named, we ought to introduce Dickens's Silas Wegg, whose "favourite book" was "The Decline and Fall Off" of the Roman Empire. The opinions of characters in fiction are of no value in a critical work.

"Boswell's intemperance . . . at last carried him off." This is not known—or at least cannot be known. He died of an intermitting fever. Johnson said of "hospitals and other public institutions," that all the good is done by one man, who drives on the others. To illustrate this, Dr B. Hill quotes Fielding, on the "difficulty of *getting admission*" into hospitals.

Johnson, we are assured, made less money because "he never traded on his reputation. When he had made his name, he almost ceased to write." Let us see. Johnson, it will be conceded, "made his name" by his Dictionary, published in 1755; but since then what a number of works he issued—the *Idler*, "Rasselas," editions of Shakespeare, "The Lives of the Poets," besides innumerable pamphlets, essays, reviews, dedications, etc. His pen was never idle a moment. We even find him eager to edit a huge Cyclopædia—a regular trade job.

Johnson said that "Hell is paved with good intentions," on which the editor quotes from Malone a passage of Herbert's, "Hell is full of good meanings." He might have gone further back, and told us that the original saying was St Bernard's.

Johnson told Hawkins that he never could see the least resemblance between a picture and its subject. "This, however," insists the editor, "must have been an exaggeration," for these reasons: Firstly, because he exhorted Sir Joshua to paint, not on "perishable canvas," but on copper! Secondly, that if a room were hung round with paintings, their faces to the wall, he would not turn them to look at them. Still nothing to do with seeing a likeness. Further, did he not buy prints, portraits of his friends, and hang them up? How does this prove that he could not see a resemblance? And the pictures he would not "turn" were described as paintings in general, not portraits; and the prints he bought were reminders of his friends, which he would like to have, even though he could not see the likeness.

On the familiar Scriptural passage, "he that smiteth thee on the one cheek," etc., the editor says, "Had Miss Burney thought of this text, she might have quoted it with effect against Johnson when he told her that 'the one' was Scotch, not English." Now, this is not in Boswell's work at all; and so far from its "being quoted with effect" against Johnson, he would have replied, "And what then, ma'am? The translators had used a Scotch expression." As it happens, Boswell used the words "one cheek," not "the one cheek," so the anecdote has no application at all.

VII.

Johnson spoke to Mrs Piozzi of his man Frank, and described how "a female haymaker had followed him to London for love." "Here," says the editor, "Mrs Piozzi shows her usual inaccuracy. The visit was paid early in the year, and was over in February. *What haymaking*," asks Dr B. Hill impressively, "*was there in that season?*" No haymaking, of course; but Johnson was describing the ordinary profession of the woman, as though he might say "a hop-picker," or "a harvest-man," without regard to the time. Moreover, in his eagerness to correct, the editor overlooks Johnson's phrase, "followed him to London," which might have been after a long or short interval, and in the haymaking season. These are trivialities, and it is a trivial thing setting trivial things right; but why introduce them? When at Monboddo's, Johnson took up his large oaken stick, and said, "My lord, that's *Homeric*," thus pleasantly alluding to his lordship's favourite writer. The editor has this odd fancy: "Perhaps he was referring to Polyphemus's club," which is then described as being as large as a mast; or to "Agamemnon's *sceptre*." This is being altogether too literal. Johnson surely had no special passage in his mind; he was taking a liberal, general view. He said that his stick was Homeric, as he would say a feast was Homeric, or a contest was Homeric. Every one understands this.

When Johnson went to see the English chapel at Montrose, he gave "a shilling extraordinary" to the clerk. The reason of this *largesse*, the editor opines, was that he found the church so much cleaner than others. But Johnson, as he gave the coin, gave also the reason: "He belongs to an honest church"—that is, to his own church. Clear enough.

The verses "Every island is a prison," the

editor tells us, are by "*a* Mr Coffey." Can he be unaware that "*a* Mr Coffey" was a well-known, popular dramatist, author of many pieces, notably of "The Devil to Pay," one of Mrs Clive's most popular pieces?

Speaking of Boswell's portrait, the editor says "it was given to him by Sir J. Reynolds." No; it was commissioned by Boswell, who contracted to pay for it after a fixed time. We are rather astonished to learn that the Greek compound word ευμελιης means "armed with good ashen spear." There is no suggestion of "spear" or "armed." It appears to mean "of good ash" simply. Boswell speaks of Adam Smith's defence of Hume as being still prefixed to his "History of England," "like a list of quack medicines sold by the same bookseller." The editor says that the bookseller was Francis Newbery; but the publisher of the "History" was Millar, not Newbery, as Boswell elsewhere states.

Johnson wrote to his printer on October 14, 1776, saying, "I sent you some copy." "The copy, or MS.," the editor explains, "I conjecture," was certain "proposals" for a work on "Erse" that Mr Shaw was publishing. When an author writes to a printer, "I sent you *some* copy," he generally means a portion of copy, or some of the MS.; but this is only a complete scrap of some twenty-five lines. As he had discharged his duty in writing, and supplied the "proposals," he would not write to complain, "I have sent you some copy, but you have not noticed it." But the whole discussion arises out of "a letter about copy," which is not in Boswell's book at all.

We learn with some astonishment that "Johnson did not generally print his name" on his works, for he published anonymously "Lobo's Abyssinia," "London," "The Life of Savage," the *Rambler* and *Idler*, "Rasselas," and four pamphlets. To other works he did put his name. Let us take this list and see. "Lobo" was a translation, and a piece of "hack work" which he was ashamed of. The *Rambler* and *Idler* were periodicals, to which it was not usual to attach the authors' names. Moreover, he was assisted by friends. The pamphlets were political, and pamphlets were nearly always issued anonymously; but when they were collected in a volume, Dr B. Hill admits that he *did* put his name. In the case of "The Life of Savage" there were obvious reasons for concealing the author's name, as it involved a piece of delicate family history. There remain only "Rasselas" and the "London." In the case of the latter, he concealed the author's name even from the publisher; and he was, moreover, at the time an obscure drudge whose name was of no account. As to "Rasselas," I confess I can find no reason for concealment. But I ask, is Dr B. Hill justified in saying that "Johnson did not *generally* put his name to his books," especially as he did put his name to his most notable books—the Dictionary, "Lives of the Poets," etc.?

Some of the editor's explanations of the most simple matters are truly extraordinary, and presume an almost childish innocence in his readers. When Boswell tells us that the Ministers suppressed certain passages in the proof sheets of Johnson's pamphlet, the editor furnishes a letter of Johnson's, in which he writes to the printer, "Print me half a dozen copies in the original state." But the too conscientious editor must explain: "When Johnson writes, 'When you print it, print me,' etc., he uses, doubtless, 'print' in the sense of *striking off copies*. The pamphlet was, we may assume, in type before it was revised. The corrections had been made in the proof sheets. Johnson asks to have six copies." Surely every one knows the distinction between composing, or "setting up," and "printing." And all this needless comment on a letter not in Boswell's book at all! In the same spirit a trivial direction of Johnson's—also not in Boswell—is dealt with. He asked that "a copy be franked to me." "Mr Strahan had a right, as a Member of Parliament, to frank all letters and packets. *That is to say, by merely writing his signature in the corner, he could pass them through the post free of charge.*" But should an editor supply such comments as these?

Boswell wrote to the Royal Academy that he was proud to be a member of an institution to which, as it had "the peculiar felicity of not being dependent on a Minister, but was under the immediate patronage of the Sovereign," he would do his best to be of service. Here Dr B. Hill morbidly fancies that Boswell is aiming a stroke at Pitt! "See *post* for Boswell's grievances against Pitt." Nothing could be more far-fetched. Boswell was simply referring to the unusual constitution of the Academy, which was a Royal institution, and emphasising his own loyalty. He was speaking generally. The idea that he would sneer at the king's favourite minister, when addressing the king's institution, is absurd.

The editor often seems to claim a prior discovery, on the ground that what he writes "was in type" before some piece of information was imparted to him. We, of course, may accept his statement; but, technically speaking, once a statement is printed, no such claim can avail. Thus, speaking of George Psalmanazar being at Oxford, he had "conjectured" that he had stayed at Christ Church, but "since this Appendix was in type I have learned, through the kindness of Mr Doble, what confirms my conjecture"; and the Doble authority is then quoted. But Dr B. Hill knew it before.

The editor assures us that "*bon-mots that are miscarried*, of all kinds of good things, suffer the most." Miscarried, in this sense, "is *not* in Johnson's Dictionary," and is a verb neuter. A *bon-mot* may miscarry, but is not *mis*carried.

One of Dr B. Hill's proofs of Johnson's love of travelling is that "he was pleased with Martin's account of the Hebrides." While discussing this matter, the editor strangely pauses to give an account of the populations of particular towns. "So late as 1781, Lichfield had not 4000 inhabitants. Birmingham, I suppose, had not so many. Its growth was wonderfully rapid. Between 1770 and 1797," and so on. In this connection, too, he insists a good deal on Johnson's 'living with the Thrales, and seems to reckon his repeated visits to Streatham as "travels." Then he calculates that Johnson "must have seen all the cathedrals of England"; but he excepts one, for some mysterious reason. "Hereford, I think, he could not have visited." And why not? It was not very far from Lichfield, and on his road to Wales he was likely enough to have passed it. Then we are told that Lichfield is described as "the city and county of Lichfield" in a certain "Tour of Great Britain." Boswell does not mention this important fact, nor care about it; but the editor, having mentioned this "Tour," informs us that "Balliol College has a copy of the work"; further, that the copy displays "Garrick's book-plate"; further again, the book-plate exhibits "Shakespeare's head at the top of it," and some lines from "Menagiana," which are duly quoted!

Boswell alludes to the "Memoir of Whitehead," of which the editor tells us that he "had long failed to find a copy," though he searched the Bodleian, the British Museum, the London, Cambridge, and Advocates' Libraries. "Searched"—that is, consulted the catalogues. But the book is not what is called "rare," and a real search among the second-hand booksellers would to a certainty have procured it. As it turned out, there was a copy in Mr Forster's library at South Kensington, which leads to compliments, well deserved no doubt, to the obliging gentleman who had charge of it. But these thanks and explanations about finding or not finding old books are a waste of words and space, and have nothing to do with the editing of Boswell, who himself dismissed the topic as "a sneering observation," which was quite enough.

In a copy of the "Life," which belonged to Wilkes, and which I have had in my hands, is a curious marginal note on the passage where Johnson is described as withdrawing from "behind the scenes," and as giving a very broadly expressed reason for his withdrawal. This little anecdote was told to Boswell by Hume, who had it from Garrick. In Wilkes's note a much coarser phrase is given, which the discoverer could not bring himself to print. The editor eagerly defends Johnson. Had he not declared "that obscenity was always repressed in his presence"? Garrick, no doubt, "was restrained *by some principle*, some delicacy of feeling." (Poor Garrick!) "It is possible that he reported the very words to Hume, and that Hume did not change them. It is idle to dream that they can now be *conjecturally amended.*" Now, on this I will remark that the editor here confounds —as he does in other places—"obscenity" with coarseness. The speech, even as recorded by Boswell, is surely coarse enough, and I hesitate even to copy it here. What is there so improbable in its having been still coarser? And I think that any one nicely critical will see that Boswell has attempted to soften the phrase by some sort of periphrasis which is not Johnsonian. Again, Wilkes wrote his pencilled note, not for publication, but for his own private use, and to correct a mistake; and it is exactly the sort of story that would have attraction for him, and which he would recollect.

Speaking of the old woman in the Hebrides, Boswell tells us that Johnson would insist on seeing her bed-chamber, "like *Archer* in 'The Beaux's Stratagem.'" Now this is a very gay and happy illustration, when we think of the old crone and her hovel. The editor says gravely, "Boswell refers, I think, to a passage in act iv. sc. 1: 'I can't at this distance distinguish the figures of the embroidery.'" He may well say, "I think," for no one else could see any connection between the passages. Boswell had said nothing about "the embroidery." He "refers," of course, to what comes before: "I suppose 'tis your ladyship's bed-chamber." The editor then, *en passant*, offers the odd hypothesis that Goldsmith had plagiarised the passage! "This is copied in 'She Stoops to Conquer'—'So, then, you must show me your embroidery.'" Astonishing! *Marlow* asks simply, "Do you work, child?" then asks to see her embroidery. Not a word about the chamber. And so Boswell having spoken of an old woman and her hut, we find ourselves straying off to "embroidery" and Goldsmith.

Dr B. Hill tells us that "in twenty years the number of children received into the Foundling Hospital amounted to about 15,000, of which over 8000 had died." He adds, "a great many of them died, no doubt, after they had left the Hospital." Why "no doubt"? It is clear the return refers, in both instances, to the time of residence. Returns of such a character have no meaning or value outside the institution with which they are concerned. It is a truism to assume that many die after leaving a school or an institution.

Johnson wrote the rather imaginative parliamentary reports for the *Gentleman's Magazine* for a certain time; and when he found they were taken to be genuine, gave up the task. Dr B. Hill fills an Appendix of twelve closely printed pages with his researches on the point. Wishing to show the risks Johnson ran in publishing such reports, the editor introduces one Cooley, who printed a pamphlet against "The Embargo," in which he charged the Members of the House with jobbery, and which he gave away at the door to every Member. The House voted this paper a scandalous and malicious libel, and sent printer and author to jail. The editor would have us believe that Johnson and Cave, in issuing their fanciful sketches of the debates, were incurring the same dangers! There was no likeness in the cases. But Cooley's *brochure* furnishes the editor with this digression:—"Adam Smith had just gone up, a young man, to Oxford; and there are considerations in this paper" (of Cooley's) "which the great authority of the author of 'The Wealth of Nations' had not yet made pass current as truth." That is, and in less stately language, there is an anticipation of some of Smith's doctrines. "He" (Cooley) "was in knowledge a hundred years before his time, and was made to suffer." And for what? For grossly insulting the members of the House of Commons, and distributing his libel at the door! We further learn, to our astonishment, that these sham debates of Johnson's "are a monument to the greatness of Walpole and the genius of Johnson. Had he *not* been overthrown, the people *would have called for these reports, even though Johnson had refused to write them.*" Thus Dr B. Hill settles everything in his own way—how it ought to have happened, and must have happened. Who can tell what "the people" would have done?

Dr B. Hill is fond of minutely explaining technical terms connected with printing, etc. Thus he tells us that "copy is manuscript for printing." So it is, no doubt; but this is not an exact definition, for any paper that is given to the printer to "set up" is "copy." It may be printed, or type-written. The great bulk of Dr B. Hill's own six volumes—or rather, Boswell's—was "set," not from "manuscript for printing," but from "copy," that is, from the printed third edition.

There is something very droll in the following:—"The Rev. J. Hamilton Davies tells me *that he entirely disbelieves* that Baxter said that Hell was paved with infant skulls." Of what value to any one is it to be told that a Rev. J. Hamilton Davies "tells" some one that he disbelieves so and so?

"Depend upon it," said Johnson, "no woman is the worse for sense or knowledge." The editor must show that here the sage contradicts himself—for "see *post,* where he says, 'Supposing a wife to be of a studious or argumentative turn, it would be very troublesome.'" Any one can see that there is no inconsistency. In the first case Johnson spoke of "sense" and "knowledge"; in the last of her pursuing study to the neglect of duty, or disputing with her husband, which are wholly different.

Here are some of those imaginary coincidences in which the editor delights:—"August 15—Mr Scott came to breakfast." "*Sir Walter Scott was two years old this day.*" Why select "*this* day"? Is it because Mr Scott's, the lawyer's, name was mentioned? The following year Sir Walter would have been three years old "that day," and so on. Further, when Johnson and Boswell returned to Edinburgh, "*Jeffrey was living, a baby then seventeen days old.*" And at Lochness, we are told, "the travellers must have passed close to the cottage where Sir J. Mackintosh *was living,* a child of seven." When Johnson matriculated in

December, 1728, we are told that "Rousseau left Geneva, and so entered upon his eventful career. Goldsmith was born eleven days after Johnson entered. Reynolds was five years old. Burke was born before Johnson left Oxford," etc. This list, it is obvious, could be extended to an inordinate length by including every one of Johnson's generation. There is no relevancy or coincidence in such things.

The editor tells us of Malone's "Life of Boswell." What is Malone's "Life of Boswell"? In Mrs Gamp's phrase, "there is no sich a book," though there is a magazine sketch by Malone.

Boswell relates that they "saw Roslin Castle and the beautiful Gothic chapel." Now, had the editor gone off to the Topographical Dictionaries, and given long extracts as to the antiquatics, etc., we should have felt no surprise, for 'tis his way. But he prefers to speculate on his own account. "Perhaps *the same woman* showed the chapel twenty-nine years later, when Scott visited it." No one can care, nor does it in the least matter. But as we *are* speculating, these points must be considered: (1) Johnson's guide may not have been a woman; (2) there may have been no guide at all; (3) after some thirty years it is unlikely that the same guide was there; (4) Boswell, who would certainly have recorded Johnson's talk with the guide, does not mention one.

After the '45, one Malcolm, we are told, thought himself in such danger of conviction that "he would have gladly compounded for banishment." Could anything be clearer? Government often made such terms with rebels. But says the editor, "By banishment he means, I conjecture, *transportation as a convict slave* to the American plantations."

Johnson wrote, "I am sorry you *was* not gratified," etc. The word is found in all the editions. It was, as the editor assures us, a common form with authors of the time; yet he says, "I doubt greatly if Johnson ever so expressed himself." Johnson, however, uses it on several other occasions in his "talk." Why not accept it? "It is strange," says the editor, in his favourite phrase, "that Boswell does not mention that on this day they met the Duke and Duchess of Argyle in the street. Perhaps the Duchess showed him the same coldness," etc. That this at least could not be the reason is clear; for they also met Mr and Mrs Langton, and Boswell does not mention *them*. Boswell's task was to record his friend's conversations, etc., and Johnson mentions other particulars which are not alluded to by Boswell.

Boswell found Johnson "in no very good humour," after Mrs Thrale had gone to Bath on the death of her child; "yet," says the editor in wonder, "he wrote to Mrs Thrale next day, and called on Thrale," and wrote yet again to Mrs Thrale. Johnson was indeed for the moment a little "put out," because he had had his journey for nothing; but the editor must fancy that he was seriously offended, would not write, etc.; and it is taking but a petty view of Johnson's character. "No very good-humour" is a different thing from taking offence.

Johnson once said, speaking of some mediæval period, "A Peer would have been angry to have it thought that he could not write his name." "Perhaps," says the editor, "Scott had this saying of Johnson in his mind when he made Earl Douglas exclaim," etc. The idea that Scott, who had at his fingers' ends all the lore of the times, should be indebted to "a saying of Johnson's" for so trite a fact, is out of the question.

There is an unfinished letter of Langton's, written on the night of Johnson's death; and Langton, it is assumed, was so filled with horror that he could not finish it. This is all melodramatic, and has no foundation. Johnson died about seven o'clock in the evening. All we know is that Langton wrote his letter in the room, and that at eleven he called upon Hawkins to tell him this story. He might have come from his own house.

Again, we find the editor actually discussing a very trivial point that arose between Mr Croker and the *Gentleman's Magazine*. The *Gentleman's Magazine* had said that none but a convict could have written Dodd's sermon to the convicts, and Mr Croker fancied that this was meant offensively to Johnson. Dr B. Hill then gravely vindicates this writer in the *Gentleman's Magazine*:—"*He* knew that it" (the sermon) "was delivered in the chapel by a prisoner under sentence. If instead of 'written' he had said 'delivered,' *his meaning would have been quite clear.*" Who cares for this writer in the *Gentleman's Magazine*, or whether his meaning might have been made "quite clear" or the reverse? But this suggested change would actually destroy the point of the remark, such as it is; for its effect was from its being supposed to be the *composition* of the convict.

Johnson, speaking of Dodd, said "as soon as the King signed his sentence,"etc. But the editor tells us that "the King signs no sentence or death-warrant"; a report is brought to him, and he assents or dissents. But this amounts to signing a sentence. That Johnson was using a figure is evident from the word "sentence," which is the Judge's province.

Boswell says that the delay in issuing his great work was caused by his friends not sending in their contributions; but the editor tells us it was "in part due to Boswell's dissipation and place-hunting." The instances given amount to no more than a few evenings lost by dinner parties, which put off the revision for those evenings; and the "place-hunting" was an interruption of three weeks caused by his attending Lord Lonsdale to the North. And this is all, out of the five years and more during which Boswell was engaged on the work! Thus the editor magnifies things.

The editor has an *idée fixe* that if there be a slight misdescription of a personage in a story, the whole must collapse. Thus Northcote told how he had heard that Johnson was once intoxicated, when he said, "Sir Joshua, it is time to go to bed." The editor finds that Sir Joshua was not knighted at the time: "One part of this story is wanting in accuracy, *and therefore all may be untrue.*" This is surely an uncritical canon. Again, when Hawkins was still a member, Johnson said of him, "Sir John, sir, is a very unclubable man." The editor thinks that, as Hawkins was not knighted at the time, "the anecdote, being proved to be inaccurate on one point, may be inaccurate on another, and may therefore belong to a later time." Wrong in a trifle, you must be wrong in an important matter.

"A celebrated infidel wit" was mentioned, of whom it was said, "*Il n'a esprit que contre Dieu.*" The editor thinks that this was the comparatively obscure Fitzpatrick! Observe, he is "celebrated" and "infidel," and celebrated from exercising his wit on the subject of the Almighty. Is all this known of Fitzpatrick? Then we are told, "there are lines in the 'Rolliad' *bordering* on profanity." But though Fitzpatrick wrote in the "Rolliad," are *these* by him? and is *bordering* on profanity the same as "*l'esprit contre Dieu*"?

Boswell had written enthusiastically his delight that Auchinleck was near an English Cathedral; and Johnson sensibly bade him remember that it was some hundred and fifty miles away. The editor says, "It was not half that distance away." Any one can see by the map that Auchinleck is over a hundred and fifty miles from Chester. But Boswell was writing both of Chester and Carlisle Cathedrals, and Johnson thought he had referred to Chester Cathedral.

Here is an instance of singular perversion of meaning. Gibbon's hostile feeling towards Boswell was, it seems, so marked that, though he names eighteen members of the Literary Club as "a constellation of British stars," he leaves Boswell out. Now (1) these eighteen selected names were the very foremost in letters and art —Johnson, Burke, Goldsmith, etc.; (2) Boswell had then written only the "Hebrides," and in no case could he be included in "a large and luminous constellation of British stars"; and (3) in the very line before, Gibbon actually refers to Boswell's "Tour," p. 97, for a suitable description of this very Literary Club! Speaking of women's learning, Johnson said that "if a wife were of a studious or argumentative turn, it would be very troublesome." "*Yet*," says the editor, "*he gave lessons in Latin* to Miss Burney and Miss Thrale." There is no point in this odd "yet." Johnson was speaking of the *perversion* of such learning.

Even in the editor's acknowledgments of assistance there is a "high-falutin" tone that is out of place. When the courteous Mr Fortescue, of the British Museum, is introduced, why should we hear of "the *spacious room* over which he so worthily presides"? The librarian of his own college had the "kindness" to allow him, it seems, "to make a careful examination of Johnson's MSS."—a favour extended as of course to any literary man. It appears, however, that he never took his eyes off the editor when at his work; and this "vigilance," he is certain, will ensure that the college will never have to "mourn the loss of a single leaf." This surely was not worth mentioning.

The first edition of "Cocker," the editor tells us, "was published about 1660." Now, this is a trivial matter, and has nothing to do with Boswell or Johnson; but it may be as well stated correctly. Cocker's first work on the subject was published in 1669—that is, his "Decimal Arithmetic"; but the book Johnson gave to the maid-servant was the "Arithmetic: a Plain and Familiar Method," which was published in 1678. Brunet and Lowndes agree in this date. The editor adds: "*Though* he" (Johnson) "says that a book of science is inexhaustible, *yet* in the *Rambler* he asserts that the principles of arithmetic and geometry may be understood in a few days." Surely to understand the *principles* of a science in a few days is a different thing from "exhausting" that science!

The editor tells us that Boswell welcomed Paoli on his arrival in London, in September 1769. This must be all wrong, he thinks; for Wesley, being at Portsmouth on October 13, missed seeing the General, who had "just landed in the docks." I suspect the editor thinks that "landed" meant "landed in England" from Corsica.

At Lord Errol's house Johnson spoke "in favour of entails," so that noble families should not "fall into indigence." "Perhaps," the editor speculates, "the *poverty of their hosts* led to this talk"; and he quotes Sir Walter Scott, who said that "improvidence had swallowed up the estate of Errol." Now, first, the Earl's brother was present, and "the poverty of their hosts" would not be likely to lead to so awkward a subject in his presence (for Boswell distinctly states that Mr Boyd was absent only when Johnson recited the ode "*Jam satis*"); secondly, Scott was speaking of 1814, close on *forty* years later.

JOHNSON'S STAY AT OXFORD.

HERE is a very interesting, much-debated question: How long was Johnson at the University? The popular notion, always accepted after the account given by his friends and contemporaries, is that he really completed his term, but left without taking a degree. Mr Croker, however, on inspecting the books, was the first to broach a theory that he had been only fourteen months at Oxford. After an interval of nearly sixty years, Dr B. Hill is found to adopt the theory; so does the Rev. Mr Napier, so does Mr Birrell, and so does the editor of the Globe edition. All these editors seems to think that there can be no dispute about the point. But on the other side, who have we? Boswell himself, the friend and biographer; Hawkins, friend, biographer, and executor; Murphy, another friend and biographer; contemporary accounts and memoirs; I may add myself and my edition, because I was the first since Mr Croker to investigate the matter afresh at the fountain-head. Finally, Mr Leslie Stephen, a sound Johnsonian, inclines to the three years' theory.

Boswell announces in the most positive way that Johnson "left the college in autumn, 1731, without a degree, having been a member of it little more than three years." Now, that painstaking writer has told us "that I have sometimes been obliged to run half over London in order to fix a date correctly; which, when I had accomplished, I well knew would obtain me no praise, though a failure would have been to my discredit." Here is a date, year, and month, and a period given, for which he had no need to "run half over London" to ascertain, for he had simply to consult his great friend, or his great friend's tutor, Dr Adams. And he actually tells us that on several occasions he obtained from Johnson all the particulars of his early life and education. Further, once at Oxford, Boswell extracted from Dr Adams everything about Johnson's residence at Oxford. Would not his first question have been: "And how many years, sir, did he remain there?" It is quite impossible to put aside the force of this argument.

Again, we should consider the number of details and events that have come down to us of Johnson's college life, his acquaintances, poverty, studies, and change of tutors, etc., all of which suggest a regular University course, quite incompatible with a stay of a few months. All through his life he looked on himself and spoke of himself as a "University man," who belonged to the place, which he certainly would not have done had he been there only fourteen months. Would he have been constantly returning and stopping there, and calling up old memories of places and friends? Any reader would have an uneasy feeling that Johnson, after so short a residence, and being obliged to quit the place under the stigma of not being able to pay his way, was making but a pretence of being an Oxonian. He would be really little more than a "freshman." Nay, those fourteen months would have been but too painful an episode for Johnson himself to recall, and he would certainly have shunned all allusion to his Alma Mater. Further, would the University have given him two degrees on so slender a connection?

Next for Hawkins, the much maligned. He was an old friend of Johnson's; he attended him on his death-bed, he prepared his will, acted as his executor, wrote his life, and edited his works. He, therefore, ought to have known something about Johnson. Not only does he know something, but he furnishes minute and particular details about his Oxford life. He tells that as it would have been impossible for the humble bookseller to support his son at Oxford, it was arranged that he should go as a sort of assistant in his studies to a Mr Andrew Corbet, the son of a Shropshire gentleman, and one of his schoolfellows. He was to be with him "in the character of a companion," and his college charges were to be defrayed by him. Boswell heard this story also, but he says it was too delicate a matter to question his friend upon. Dr Taylor, however, told him that Johnson "never received any assistance whatever" from the Corbets. This, however, would seem to be owing to the abrupt termination of the arrangement, for after nearly two years' stay, or it may be fourteen months, young Corbet quitted the college. Hawkins adds that all he could obtain was that the father of the young man should continue to pay for his commons. Then the knight makes this distinct and positive statement: "The time of his continuance at Oxford is divisible into two periods, the former whereof commenced on the 31st day of October, 1728, and determined in December, 1729, when, as appears by a note in his 'Diary' in these words: '1629, Dec. S. J. Oxonio rediit,' he left this place, the reason whereof was a failure of pecuniary supplies from his father; but meeting with another source, the bounty, it is supposed, of some one or more of the members of the cathedral, he returned and made up the whole of his residence—about three years." Hawkins, who was not so delicate as Boswell, had evidently talked the subject over with Johnson, for the latter explained to him that his father had become a bankrupt about this time. The cathedral friend was likely enough to have been the Dean, for long after Johnson "cancelled" some passages in his "Journey," which had been printed off, for fear of giving him pain, saying that he had once done him an important service. I have thought, too, that Johnson's care of Mrs Desmoulins might have been owing to some assistance of this kind received from her father, Dr Swinfen. So everything, it will be seen, points in this direction.

But now for the argument from the "Battels," or, I suppose, Buttery Books, which are the entries of commons supplied to the students there. These reports I may take credit for being the first to publish, the late Professor Chandler having had them copied for me. From the time of Johnson's entrance in October, 1728, to December, 1729, the entries in these books are continued regularly week by week, and small charges are placed opposite his name. After that date there sets in a state of great capriciousness and irregularity, to be explained by the capricious irregularity of Johnson's own situation. True, in December, 1729, Johnson makes that entry of his return home from Oxford, to which appeal is made as showing that his career was closed, and that it agrees exactly with the cessation of the charges for meals. But this is almost at once demolished by our finding that on January 30, 1730, there is a charge of 5d.; so that, though we are told that he had left Oxford for good, and closed his course, we find him back again! Now this 5d. is rather significant. We are assured that "Battels" is evidence of residence, and that every one who resides must have the meals of which the "Battel Books" are records. But here we have Johnson at the college, yet having only 5d. worth of food or drink. His meals or meal must, therefore, have been charged to some one else. Further, his name now figures regularly in the books, week after week, though there are no charges. Then comes another surprise. On March the 13th we find him paying for a week's meals, 4s. 7d., and on March 27th, 5d.; so this represents a fortnight's stay at least. I believe the explanation is that he was absent at Lichfield for the first two months of the year trying to make some arrangement, and that on his return he paid for a week's commons or so. At all events, here he is shown to be still at Oxford, three months after he is supposed to have finally left. This accounts for some eighteen months. His name is now entered regularly week after week, still without charges, down to November 27, 1730, when it is removed altogether for nearly two months, to reappear once on January 29, 1731, but without charges. This removal might show that he had gone away finally, and had lost hope of returning. But the name again reappears on March 12, 1731, and is continued steadily, without charges, down to October 1, when it finally vanished, the three years claimed being all but completed. What explanation can be given of these fitful disappearances and replacings, except that the unhappy youth was now remaining struggling desperately to retain his footing, now hurrying away to obtain aid, now succeeding or failing; that he was at the college, but that his meals were charged to some one else? No other rational reason can be given of Johnson's name being withdrawn from the books altogether, and then restored, save that the few charges set down were of his own payment, and that the blanks meant that the charge was defrayed in some other way. Had he gone away altogether, his name would have been summarily removed. This absence of charges for meals when he was in residence points to surely some eleemosynary system of assistance, to some charging to another person's account. Mr Elwin thinks that the college supplied him gratis, and held over the charges till better times. Dr B. Hill thinks this impossible—that the charges for meals must be the only evidence of residence; but this, as I have shown, is disposed of by those entries where only 5d. is charged, from which it is evident he was in residence, and yet is not charged with his meals. Dr B. Hill thinks, too, that when the name is given week after week, it was merely kept on the books in the hope of his return; but on this theory how is it to be explained that the name is given in the very first entry after he had arrived at the University, and this without any charges opposite to it? I think, therefore, that this argument from the "Battels," fails.

There is an entry in the books that Johnson's "caution money," £7, was forfeited to satisfy a claim of the college for monies owing to the college for that amount. As Mr Macleane, the recent historian of Pembroke College, points out, it is improbable that the debt and caution money could exactly balance each other, so that Johnson may have owed much more. Now, this seems to support the argument, and proves, at the least, that the college was giving him credit for his "Battels"; and that principle once established, it is not difficult to go further.

Dr Adams, as we know, was Johnson's tutor. On his entrance, one Mr Jordan was his tutor, but about the middle of 1730 this gentleman left the college, and Dr Adams succeeded him. He was given a living early that year, and it seems almost certain that Dr Adams would have taken over his pupils after the long vacation of 1730.

Giving Boswell information about Johnson's college life, Dr Adams said to him that he was his nominal tutor, which Boswell, in a contradictory passage, interprets to mean that he *would* have been his tutor had Johnson returned to the college. This, however, it is clear, was not Adams' meaning, for he added, "I was his nominal tutor, but he was above my mark;" and Johnson, when the remark was repeated to him, accepted this meaning, saying it was a noble and generous speech.

It has been said, however, that this demolishes the argument for Johnson's longer stay, for, if he remained till 1731, Adams would have been more than his nominal tutor. He would have been his tutor for two years. The answer to which is that Boswell made a mistake as to the year of Adams' taking over Jordan's pupils, which, as Dr B. Hill shows, was at the end of 1730 and not in 1731. This, it seems to me, completely disposes of the argument as to the "*would* have been his tutor had Johnson returned"; for even on the supposition that Johnson only remained fourteen months, Adams would have been his actual and not nominal tutor for several months of that period.

This rather damaging fact the editor seems to pass by. Observe his argument was that Johnson was never under Adams at all. But "this," says the editor, "is no contradiction of the statement that Adams was only Johnson's nominal tutor. The exercises were often performed in the hall, no doubt, before the Masters and Fellows." "Why, sir, what sophistry is this?" as the sage would say. "*Before* the Masters and Fellows," says the editor. No doubt this was so; but Johnson says that he "performed" before them "under" Adams, that is, prepared and directed by him. It is astonishing that such a plea should be made.

Then there is Dr Taylor's part of the case. Dr Taylor, as we know, was one of Johnson's oldest friends—also his life-long friend. Johnson told Mrs Piozzi that the history of all his Oxford exploits lay between Taylor and Adams—a large phrase, by the way, that seems to speak of a long period in which these exploits were performed. Taylor told Boswell the incident of Johnson's ceasing to visit him at Christ Church College, from shame at his own poverty-stricken appearance. That they were at Oxford there can be no doubt. Yet Taylor entered in June, 1730, some months after Johnson, according to the short-stay theorists, had quitted it, which would prove convincingly—there is no getting over it—that Johnson was there after June, 1730. All Dr B. Hill can do is to say that "this seems at first sight to follow, but we must remember that Taylor *might* have had his name entered some months before he came, and that after his name was entered Johnson might have left." What this means it is impossible to guess; it does not alter the fact that Johnson and Taylor were there together, and the former in the habit of visiting him at Christ Church. He has at last to throw up his case, "nevertheless, the whole story is very strong evidence that Johnson was in residence in the latter half of the year 1730." Dr B. Hill, however, discovered another Dr J. Taylor, who entered about the same time as Johnson, and he contends that he was Johnson's friend.

The most perplexing element in the controversy is the case of Whitfield. Boswell calls him Johnson's "fellow collegian," and he reports Johnson as saying that he was at the same college with him and knew him before he became better than other people. Now, Whitefield only entered in 1732, when it is admitted, even by advocates of the long stay, that Johnson had left. It will be seen it is a crux for both sides. I do not profess to be able to solve the question, but these points are worthy of consideration. First, as to the meaning of "fellow collegian." "His fellow collegian," used by Boswell, may certainly imply, without much forcing of the meaning, "belonging to the same college," without any regard to the time of residence. If Johnson said "Whitfield was at my college," Boswell may have thought he meant at the same time. Later, Boswell reports the phrase about Whitfield being at the same college with him, to which he (Boswell) may have given the same meaning, of belonging to the same college. But then Johnson adds that he knew him before he became better than other people. And it was at college—say about 1733—that he became "better than other people." But this Dr B. Hill and his supporters have not noticed. How came it to pass that the clerks of the Buttery Books would continue for two years entering the name of a *non-resident* in this pertinacious and regular way, as though he were a member of "the mess," as it were, but never attended? Would they not have suspended their entries as time rolled on? What, it might be asked, had they to do with the list of persons on the college books? All they were concerned with were the persons who were supplied with college victuals. As it happens, they *did* leave off entering his name, for short periods, so we are asked to believe that these clerks would go periodically to the authorities to remove, or put on again, according to the entries of the college books, the name of a person to whom they supplied nothing in their department. It would be now "Johnson is off the books," and now "Johnson is on." "But he is never here—has never been here for two years—and gets nothing from us." Then, with all the personal investigations of these ledgers by Dr Chandler and Dr B. Hill, they have never discovered another case of the kind, that is, where a student remains away from the college, but has his name on the Buttery list with blanks opposite to it.

Another strong proof of the longer stay is Dr Adams' declaration that he was "his nominal tutor"—*i.e.* that after the three years, in 1731, he had succeeded Jordan, and would have been Johnson's tutor had the latter returned. This surely is an indication that, up to that period, Johnson was in the college. Had he left, as is contended, some two years before, Adams would not have talked of being his tutor at all, "nominal" or otherwise. Johnson's career had been long since closed; but Adams speaks clearly as though he had been at the college all the time, and thus seems to have said to Boswell that had he *returned* (after the vacation), and gone on with his studies, he would have found a new tutor.

I now resume the task and duty of pointing out Dr B. Hill's mistakes.

Johnson heartily praised Murphy's plays, giving him a high place as a dramatist. "*Yet*," says the editor, on the watch to catch him, "he said there was too much *Tig and Tirry* in one piece." Thus there was one play with which he found fault. But on turning to the passage, we find Johnson was speaking, *not* of the play itself, but of the names of the characters, which were *Tig*ranes, *Tiri*dates, etc. It was a pleasant jest. "*Yet* he said," etc. A trivial matter of this kind shows how unsafe a guide is Dr B. Hill.

We have, indeed, the sage's opinion of Dr Hill: "He was an ingenious man," he said, "but had no veracity. He was, however, a very curious observer; and if he would have been contented to tell the world no more than he knew, he might have been a very considerable man, and needed not to have recourse to such expedients to raise his reputation." This was spoken, not of our Johnsonian Dr B. Hill, but of *another* Dr Hill, who lived in Johnson days, and who was really as copious and verbose as the modern. He also might have been "a considerable man, had he been content to tell the world no more than he knew."

JOHNSON'S LETTERS AND DR BIRKBECK HILL'S NOTES.

DR B. HILL has also issued two large volumes of Johnson's letters, which, according to the advertisement, "include all the letters known to be in existence, with the exception"—and here the editor is very precise—"of a few of which it has not been possible to obtain transcripts, and of those printed in my own edition of the 'Life,'" to which exact references are given. But on surveying "my collection" what do we find? First, *reference* only to over three hundred of the letters furnished by Boswell; second, a large number of scraps of letters, and epitomes of letters, often no more than a line in length, extracted by auctioneers for their catalogues, and which are counted as letters; thirdly, Mrs Piozzi's two volumes of letters, already "collected" by her; and fourthly, various printed, scattered letters, with a number that have never been in print. The "few of which it has not been possible to obtain transcripts" no doubt refer to the Perkins and Taylor letters. While, however, he claims to have furnished an almost complete collection of all the letters "then in existence," strange to say, he begins at once to have qualms, and to our astonishment we read: "It will be shown, *I fear*, that letters which are in print have been left unnoticed, and that others which I enter as new have been already noticed." There are, it seems, garners still unswept, and Dr B. Hill has uneasy suspicions, if not a certainty, that there are stores of Johnsonian letters which were refused to him, or which he knows not of, and which it is now too late to secure.

So the book should properly be described as "A Collection of Johnson's Letters, published and unpublished, with the Dates and Places of some Letters, Extracts and Epitomes of others, taken from Auctioneers' Catalogues"; or it might be called "Letters, with Lists of Letters, Extracts and Abstracts of Letters, etc."

It is a fantastic notion, truly, that of counting as "letters"—numbering each gravely—the scraps from auctioneers' catalogues, the meagre extract or abstract furnished by Puttick or Sotheby, to pique the bidder's appetite. He tells of the weary, toilsome hours he spent in the Bodleian Library, plodding through these records to light on some such scrap as this: "1043 (the number of the letter in the series). In Messrs Sotheby & Co.'s catalogue, Aug. 21, 1872, Lot 113, is a letter of Johnson's to Mrs Strahan, postponing an invitation: 'I had forgotten that I myself had invited a friend to dine with me.'" In a sort of flutter of excitement at this new department of "*research by catalogue*," the editor feels it his duty to give severe rebuke or warning to the authorities concerned. "This labour had been greatly lightened had those catalogues which contain descriptions of autographs *been bound up separately*. As it was, *I found them scattered* among long lists, not only of books, but also of musical instruments, bins of wine, and cigars." How dreadful this! He hopes, however, that the practice will be suppressed in the near future, and he directs his admonition to other institutions as well as to the Bodleian: "If librarians would *keep these catalogues apart*, *the students of literature* and history would have at their command a great amount of curious material." So see to it, *messieurs*, the Librarians!

Johnson, he assures us, "was a great letter writer." "Johnson wrote unwillingly." Now, this would not occur to any one who considers the spontaneous style and vast number of the letters: Johnson was *always* writing letters. We might suspect that the editor had mistaken the sense of his authority. And so it proves. Johnson merely says that he found himself very "unwilling to take up a pen only to tell my friend that I am well." He admitted that he wrote, not "with difficulty"—but rather "with more difficulty than those persons who write nothing but letters." It was "not without a considerable effort of resolution that he sat down to write." The editor has completely mistaken the meaning.

But commend us to the following grotesque notion. Johnson's letters in the "Life," he says, are spoiled by their position. They lose all value and attraction owing to the superior charm of the "talk." "We hurry through them (*or even skip over them*) to arrive at the passages where the larger type and the inverted commas give signs that we shall have good talk." This is simple nonsense—the editor must pardon the word. Who experiences this feeling? We always read Johnson's letters with pleasure. They belong to the narrative; they are often answers to Boswell's letters. If the editor really does wish to "skip" them, that is his own personal affair; but he should not include every one in his "we."

Few writers of our time, indeed, can furnish such genuine entertainment as Dr B. Hill. Common editors, poor souls! in their dull, practical way present their work in business-like fashion; they are thinking of their author and of his matter. But Dr B. Hill seems possessed with a perfect *furia*; he leaps and bounds; he expends himself in the wildest, most delusive theories; he raves against dead writers, as though they were now in the flesh; as a matter of course, he assails his own idol even.

We shall begin with a rare *bonne bouche*. The editor gives a letter of Johnson's "Tetty," which he styles "the gem of *my* collection." Every one knows of Johnson's curious infatuation about this woman, who seemed to him a perfect goddess. But no one will be prepared for the extraordinary company into which the editor introduces the poor lady by way of justification against Lord Macaulay's attack. "Nevertheless, at the time of her marriage, she was *just the same age* as"—who will it be supposed?—"*Barbara, Duchess of Cleveland*, when our great historian describes her as no longer young, but *still retaining* traces of that *superb and voluptuous loveliness which*," etc. Poor Tetty and a Hampton Court beauty! were there ever such a strange concatenation? But listen to this. "*For all we know*, it was *Mrs Johnson's superb and voluptuous loveliness* which overcame the heart of the lamented Mr Porter" (who lamented *him*) "and it was *the traces of it* which overcame the young Samuel." For all we know, indeed! Garrick and Boswell, for all we *do* know, and others, have described her as a coarse, repulsive, ludicrous person. Suddenly the editor is seized with grotesque *furia*, turns on the historian, and overwhelms him with scorn, and scoffs: "She was *only a decent married woman*. *Had she been a royal harlot*, Macaulay, instead of mocking her bloom, might have laid on the colours with an art and a skill scarcely surpassed by Sir

Peter Lely." This is incoherence, and it is difficult to deal with it seriously. The reader needs not to be assured that Macaulay had no penchant for "royal harlots," nor was he their retained advocate; nor did he prefer them to "only decent married women."

Another truly rich "morsel" is connected with the death of Johnson. How is the scene to be made impressive, or, as Boswell has it, "aweful"? Why, by introducing a *stage coach!* This literally is the fact. "William Hutton, who," we are told, "left London on the night of December 12th," describes how he "went silently on over a hundred and twenty miles of snow." On which the editor adds impressively: "*As the coach went silently on through the wintry world, Johnson's spirit passed away.*" This is all solemn enough. Still, the editor ought to be accurate in his solemnity. Hutton left in his mysterious coach on the Sunday night, the 12th, and the good Johnson did not yield up his honest soul until seven o'clock on the Monday night, by which time Hutton was actually safe at home! So the whole point of the thing, such as it is, vanishes.

But we are not yet done with Hutton and his coaching.

Johnson was once returning to London through Birmingham and Oxford, when it strikes the editor as a strange coincidence that "W. Hutton took the same road *not three weeks later.*" There is something comic in the mania Dr B. Hill has for connecting Johnson and Hutton, and always in this matter of a *coach.* Without any *apropos* whatever, he proceeds to tell us all about Hutton's journey; how thirty-six horses were used: calculating "there must have been nine changes of horses in the 120 miles." We next learn how the guard sat inside with Hutton, and told him how he had defended the coach against highwaymen—sometimes had killed them, etc. We wonder what had all this to do with Johnson. But the editor thus ingeniously connects these particulars with him: "*If Johnson went by the same coach, all this talk must have been poured into the ears of Black Francis as he sat outside*"!

But "must it," after all? To be secure of even this, we must assume, first, that it was the same coach; second, the same guard; third, that the guard did tell his stories over again; and fourth, and above all, that he was sitting beside "Black Francis."

Still that does not exhaust these curious Hutton coach incidents. Johnson could not get a place in a Birmingham coach. What will be said when we find "that *nine years* later W. Hutton, returning from London, *found all the places taken,*" etc. And still more strange, "*he left in the evening of a December day.*"

There is nothing, however, in the volumes more truly comic than the following. Johnson made this simple statement:

"*I propose to come home to-morrow.*"

There are no bounds to the ingenuity of the editor; the gravest questions are here involved. How did Johnson travel? How *might* he have travelled? Above all, *had he luggage?* If he had, how did he send it? Was it heavy or light? *What did he pay?*

The editor gravely discusses all these matters. "He *might* have returned either by the Oxford coach, *which left at* 8 *a.m.—fare* 15*s.*;" and, mark this: "There were no outside passengers." Here we touch firm ground, for, of course, Johnson must have travelled inside—that is, if he did travel by this vehicle. Or did he take "'The Machine,' which left the Bear Inn every Monday, Wednesday, etc., at 6 A.M."? "The Machine" or Oxford coach? Who can tell? The editor adds resignedly: "What time these coaches *neared London* we are not told." Johnson would prefer knowing what time they *reached* London.

But there is a further important point, viz. that "'The Machine' was *not* licensed by the Vice-Chancellor." Then more details about "The Machine": It carried six inside passengers. And the serious point of *luggage*: "Each inside passenger was allowed six pounds of luggage; beyond that weight a penny a pound was charged." Bradshaw is not "in it" with all this. Still the point is left unsettled: *Had* Johnson luggage? and how much? In default of evidence, the editor does the next best thing—he speculates. "*Had Johnson sent heavy luggage*"—and how likely *that* was!—"he *might* have sent it by the university old stage waggon, which left"—and so on. And thus, bewildered by "The Machine," the "Oxford coach," the "heavy waggon," etc., we are left no wiser. I repeat, it seems incredible that any one could bring himself to write such things.

Johnson wrote from Oxford: "To-morrow, if I can, I shall go forward." The editor speculates on—no, announces positively!—the meaning of this "*if I can.*" Johnson, he says, meant that it depended on the chance of his getting a place in any of the passing coaches. Yet only in the line before is written: "But I have not been very well. I hope I am not ill by sympathy with you." This was surely what he meant by "if I can."

But let us come to one of our editor's nimblest *gambados*, and which surpasses all the rest. Johnson wrote from Ashbourne to Mrs Thrale of a letter which he had received from "Miss ——" complaining of the "frigidity with which he had answered her." She neither hoped nor desired "*to excite greater warmth.*" His salutation to her, "madam," was like a glass of cold water. "I dare neither write with frigidity *nor with fire.*" "There was formerly in France a *cour de l'amour*, but I fancy no one was ever summoned before it after threescore"; yet he would certainly be non-suited in it. "I am not very sorry that she is far off. *There can be no great danger in writing to her.*" This badinage refers to some spinster who was "making up" to the Doctor. It seems almost incredible, but the editor arrives at this amazing, bewildering solution: "*Miss Porter, I think, is meant.*" That is, Lucy Porter, his step-daughter! She was bringing him into the "Court of Love." "No great danger of his being caught in writing" to his step-daughter, to whom he was always writing. These things take one's breath away. Only three days before he had written of this very step-daughter: "Lucy is a philosopher, and considers me to be one of the external and accidental things that," etc.

Having laid down his theory, he proceeds to support it. "See *post*," he says, "where Johnson expressed his surprise that she detained him at Lichfield"—we must suppose to prosecute her plans for bringing him into the "Court of Love." Here he completely misreads the passage. On the contrary, Johnson was delighted at being pressed to stay by his Lucy. "I was pleased to find that I could please. Lucy is a very peremptory maiden." In the other "see *post*" there is the same kind of mistake: "Miss Porter will be satisfied with a very little of my company," the editor fancying here that this was a tart speech; but Johnson meant that his step-daughter would let him off after a short stay. What can be over Dr B. Hill when he writes such things?

Johnson wrote to say he had "met Mrs Langton and Juliet" at Ashbourne. Nothing could be clearer—persons, place, and incident. But the editor sees a mystery and a whole train of difficulties. "If these ladies *were* Bennet Langton's mother and sister, *they were not on the direct road to London* from the family seat in Lincolnshire." I meet my friend Smith who lives near Exeter, at Rugby: "No," our editor will say, "it could not have been Smith, because he was not on the direct road to London from his family seat." The Duke and Duchess of Argyle had been also met at the same place; so they, being out of the proper road "from the family seat," forfeit their identity! Presently we are treated to a singular speculation. As they were not Johnson's Langtons—an unusual name—Dr B. Hill suddenly discovers that "a passage in the next letter seems to show that *some actress and her daughter, or companion*, is described"! The surprises our doctor has in store for us grow and grow, and are perfectly startling. He thus proves his new point. Johnson wrote: "Mrs —— grows old, and has lost much of the undulations, etc. . . . She can act upon the stage now only for her own benefit. But Juliet is very cheerful, only lamenting the inconstancy of men." Now "Mrs ——," with the repetition of the name "Juliet," show that it refers to the same ladies. There was no actress called Langton, and Johnson was speaking with pleasant figure of "Mrs ——'s" decay when he said "she could appear only for her own benefit," while the "but" that follows, with a description of Juliet, shows that the reference to the benefit is metaphorical. Apart from this, Dr B. Hill should have noted that Johnson speaks of them as ladies of his own station. He says, "they sent for me," and "I went to them," and then he sent for Boswell to introduce him, as he had never met them. They were also known to the Thrales. In short, there can be no question they were Bennet Langton's relatives.

The editor at times indulges in a familiarity that seems rather undignified. Johnson mentioned Sir J. Mawbey, one of the House of Commons bores, on which the editor quotes the familiar lines on the Speaker:

"'There Cornwall sits, and oh, unhappy fate!
Must sit for ever, though in long debate;
Painful pre-eminence! he hears, 'tis true,
Fox, North, and Burke, but hears Sir Joseph, too.'

"*I thought, when I saw my friend, Mr Leonard H. Courtney*, sitting as chairman of committee, that to him, as member for a division of Cornwall, these lines might happily apply!" Observe, all arises out of the mere mention of Sir J. Mawbey's name. The verses might pass; but "my friend Courtney" sits for Liskeard, and therefore *Cornwall* is appropriate! And *is* it of moment to anybody what thoughts occurred to Dr B. Hill when he surveyed "my friend sitting as chairman"? Is this notion—is this friendship—is even Mr Courtney himself—of the slightest value in connection with the purpose in hand, which is the editing of Johnson's letters?

Here is a good specimen of the confusion into which Dr B. Hill's discoveries lead him. Johnson wrote to Mrs Thrale: "Invite Mr Levett to dinner" (on which, by the way, the editor remarks: "*I should not have expected* that Levett was admitted to Mrs Thrale's table," but really Johnson must have known better than Dr B. Hill). He then added: "Make enquiry what family he has, and how they proceed." Dr B. Hill refers us "for the enquiry about him," to Mrs Thrale's answer to it — and there we find her writing: "My husband bids me tell you that he has examined the register; that *Levett is only seventy-two.*" It will be seen that it is an odd answer, or no answer at all, to an enquiry "what family he has," to say "he is only seventy-two." But the editor is all astray. Johnson wished to know what "family" Levett has; that is, what persons of his own (Johnson's) household were there. This is shown by what follows, "and how *they proceed*," *i.e.* were they quarrelling, etc., as usual. Further, Johnson's letter of enquiry was dated April 18, and was from Ashbourne, and Mrs Thrale's is dated on the same day.

Thrale, wrote Johnson, to distract his grief for his son's death, said that "he would go to the house. I hope he has found something that laid hold of his attention." "*The House of Commons, I conjecture*," says our editor. Amazing! He, of course, meant the house at Southwark; the house of business, where he would find something to lay hold of his attention. But on his conjecture the editor conjectures afresh. "On April 1, *if he had attended*, he heard a debate on Mr Hartley's motion on the expenses of the American War;" and so, off we now go on a new tack. The amount of these expenses of the war Lord North could not divine. Nor could he have fancied—conjecture again—that the National Debt would have been raised from, etc., to, etc.; neither would *Gibbon* have ever, etc. That is, if Thrale *had* been there. "*For the increase of the National Debt*, see 'Penny Cyclopædia.'" And we get all this from Thrale's saying "he would go to the house." We do not know whether he ever went at all; but we get Lord North, Hartley, Gibbon, National Debt, "Penny Cyclopædia."

Dr B. Hill has a fashion of imputing degrading motives to his two heroes, when he wants to support one of his imaginary "discoveries." Sastres, "the Italian master," who was with Johnson at his death, is mentioned by Boswell, in illustration of the contrasted classes of persons with whom Johnson associated. One day he was with Colonel Fox, of the Guards, or the unhappy Levett; with Lady Crewe or Mrs Gardiner, the worthy tallow-chandler; with the Chancellor or "Sastres, the Italian master." Here Dr B. Hill morbidly sees a deliberate intention to degrade Sastres! And why? "Perhaps to punish him." And for what? "For not letting him (Boswell) publish Johnson's letters." All these assumptions are unfounded. Johnson himself in his will describes Sastres as "the Italian master"; any appreciator of Boswell's methods will feel that he introduces the name as an effective contrast; there is no proof that letters were asked for or were refused—in fact, they had been published by Mrs Piozzi—and we are asked to believe that Boswell, rich in his 300 and more letters, was infuriated because he did not obtain these five! The whole is perfect "moonshine," and, in truth, Dr B. Hill seems to *decree* a particular state of facts to suit his purpose, just as the Convention "decreed victory." So with Ryland, another correspondent of Johnson's. "Perhaps Boswell passed him over in silence in return for his keeping from him the letters he received from Johnson." As usual, there is no evidence that he refused Boswell any letters; he may have had none to refuse; as it is, only two are known. As to "passing him over in silence," what will be said when we find that Boswell, after mentioning him respectfully as one of his (Johnson's) friends, tells us that he was really unable to trace anything about him and other friends of Johnson at the time! But no. The editor will have it that Boswell was full of spite; was not Hawkesworth, Ryland's brother-in-law, a person disliked by Boswell? So, naturally, he must dislike Ryland. All which is amazing.

The occult reason for these charges is that the editor is himself very angry when any one refuses *him* the use of letters. It would seem that he could not obtain from the great brewery firm the Perkins letters—though, indeed, business houses, it is known, dislike furnishing their papers. He is scornfully indignant. "When the *secret letters and papers of kings* have been given to the world, it *might* have been thought that the private correspondence of a great scholar *with a superintendent of a brewery*," etc. It may be said there is no rule or law in these matters. People may have often good reasons for not allowing their papers to be used, even by a Dr B. Hill; and the publishing of the royal papers he speaks of are not so common as he thinks. In his anger at this disappointment he falls on the heralds, or (possibly) on the late obliging Sir B. Burke, Ulster: "I hoped to ascertain from 'The Landed Gentry' which of the descendants of the author of (Barclay's) 'Apology' purchased the great brewery, *but apparently it was thought too trifling a matter* in the history of the family to require any record." Purchasing a business is not of the importance that Dr B. Hill thinks. "The Landed Gentry" and such works give only historic details. It was, moreover, the *city* branch of the family that bought the brewery: they are named incidentally; but the head of the house who had the *landed* property is the subject of the "Landed Gentry." But to fancy poor Johnson encrusted with all this rambling comment, and, such as it is, inaccurate! It is enough to make him turn in his grave!

Indeed, there is something almost morbid in the fashion in which our editor broods over these ravished Perkins letters. They are magnified into tremendous importance. There was, he conceives, some "aweful" mystery about the "secret transactions" that passed when the brewery was sold. "Perhaps *a second hundred years* must pass away before it shall be ascertained what part Johnson took in founding the new firm." As Johnson took no part in "founding the new firm," but merely *sold* the business to them, this is likely to be unfruitful. "Still," wails the editor, "these would have thrown light *on a side of* Johnson's character that is little known." "Something, however, can even now be discovered." Providentially, as it seems, one of these "Perkins letters" got separated from the rest, and reveals part of the mystery. We now turn to it with interest, for it is always desirable to have "light thrown" on obscure questions, but are rather taken aback at finding that it is doubtful after all if it be a Perkins at all! It is only the editor's guess. And, further, it merely touches on the "iron resolution" of these executors; "Barclay's interest requires your convenience," etc. Here is not much "light." But in another place we have Dr B. Hill making this really portentous announcement, which does not throw much light on "the side of Johnson's character:" "A passage in one of Johnson's letters to Mrs Thrale *throws further light* on the *secret* transactions, by which, in the year of grace 1751, *Mr Perkins the man was changed into Mr Perkins the master.*" *Now* we shall touch firm ground. So with much curiosity we turned to the "secret transactions." Here they are: "Mr ——— came to talk about the partnership, and was very copious." (!) Such is the whole revelation.

But it seems there are other churls who possess autograph letters which they will not allow Dr B. Hill to inspect or use. Think of "the petty selfishness which makes a man *hug* some famous autograph letter *as a man hugs his gold*, rejoicing in it the more as he keeps it entirely to himself"! This is surely unreasonable. A gentleman may have paid a large price for his letter, may wish to make use of it himself, and may therefore prefer not to entrust it to Dr B. Hill.

In another work he lashes such culprits through the world. "A man who *burns* an autograph shows such an insensibility of nature, such a want of imagination, that it is likely in a more cruel age *he would have burnt heretics.*" Dickens, who had some "sensibility of nature," and whose "imagination" no one could deny, once made a vast holocaust of almost every letter he possessed, and for excellent reasons. Other eminent men have done the same thing.

We all know that the Boswell family have never felt any pride in their famous James, and seemed to wince at the recollection of his antics. Since writing—I should say noting—"The Life," Dr B. Hill determined to give these people one more chance—and approach an incorrigible old lady, Mrs Vassall, Boswell's grand-niece, who, with Caledonian bluntness, treated our doctor much as the old Lord Auchinleck treated his son. "I once tried," says our editor, "to *penetrate into Auchinleck*," a mysterious phrase, which only means that he wanted access to the library, "where I had hoped to find many curious memorials." But the owner was inexorable. As the doctor tells us, sternly and solemnly, "*Permission was refused.*" "My attempt," he adds, "had excited suspicion,"—not unnaturally; for the old lady had heard of a forthcoming edition, and that "he had some papers from Ayrshire," and "in a lady's letter begged him to be so good as to inform her from whom he had received them, and *oblige yours, etc.*" The insinuation was so obvious that the editor proceeded to make an example of the poor woman, who by this time was in her grave, holding up her methods of writing, spelling, and what not. It seems she spelt Johnson "Johnston," which is, or used to be, the correct Scotch fashion, and, what was worse, she actually directed her letter to

"G. Ber*bick* Hill, Esq."

Not to know that the great—the one Edition—had been out actually two years was bad enough; but to call *him*, the editor—"Berbick"—was too bad. He angrily stigmatised it as "contemptuous ignorance," nay, "it came to her from her father." And the woman's spelling—why, had she not written of an "Addition of Boswell"?

All which makes one think that Dr B. Hill's behaviour was not exactly chivalrous. Every touch he furnishes, I confess, only raises one's opinion of this worthy Scotch lady, who was merely exhibiting an interesting native pride of family and a natural sensitiveness.

Dr B. Hill, who is a very "nice" man, is often much shocked by Mrs Thrale's "indelicacy." When Thrale was ill Johnson was assiduous in sending excellent medical advice, of which he had a good store, and among others counselled "frequent evacuation." Allusions of this kind were customary in those days; we have since invented more delicate forms. What a woman to publish these and such-like passages! Still, "it is strange" and scarcely consistent to find the editor in one of his notes carefully informing us that Johnson, when he "took physic," meant thereby that he had "taken a purge." Fie, Dr B. Hill!

There is an extraordinary supplement labelled "Appendix B" at the end of vol. i., and which has a reference to page 14. There is, it says, among the "Hume Papers" a letter on the experiences of living at Oxford, and written by one of the Macdonald family. We are given all the dates of the writer's career, his matriculation, call to the Bar, etc. The letter is of great length, filling over two closely-printed pages. We wonder what its bearing is or what it has to do with Johnson's letters, who was at college in 1731, this being dated nigh thirty years later. We turn back, as we are invited to do, to page 14. Still no sign of relevancy—not an allusion to Oxford, or to Hume, or to Macdonald. What it means it is impossible to guess. The editor adds: "Hume had also consulted Sir Gilbert Elliot." On what? "His answers were not satisfactory." Why? Most bewildering!

Johnson wrote to Mr Thrale: "I repeat my challenge to alternate diet," which the editor strangely supposes to mean fasting on alternate days. It surely signifies alternating one kind of food with another. Dr B. Hill adds positively: "The challenge had not been given in any preceding letter." But, as, of course, he is wrong, both in his facts and in his theory, I turn, only three or four letters back, to that of April 6, and lo! we read: "Does Mr Thrale regulate himself as to regimen? Nothing can keep him so safe as the method so often mentioned. If health and reason can be preserved *by changing three or four meals a week; if such a change*," etc. There is the challenge to an "alternate diet" which our too confident editor declares does not exist; for changing three or four meals a week is not fasting on alternate days.

But here is a fresh marvel! Not satisfied with his speculations and comments, our editor must devise an imaginary text of his own—and speculate on *that*. Here are two specimens—Johnson, the editor finds, wrote: "Of flowers, if Chloris herself were here, I would present her only with the bloom of *health*." This mystifies Dr B. Hill, as well it may. He opines that if Chloris had the bloom of health, she would want nothing else. He is inclined "to conjecture" that Johnson had written "heath." Turning to the text, we find to our amazement that it is actually printed "heath"!

Johnson, in his lively vein, wrote to Mrs Thrale something about "the ladies of her rout." The editor declares that he cannot find in the great Dictionary any definition of the sense in which Johnson uses the word here. This is most extraordinary. For there Johnson explains it as "clamorous multitude," "a rabble"; that is, a noisy crowd. Could anything be clearer? Johnson was speaking of Mrs Thrale's train of gossiping, noisy females.

On two or three occasions Johnson wrote that he was getting, or had not yet got, "curiosities for Queenie's cabinet." These were little matters bought for the child when he was on his travels. The editor ponders over this; then speculates sadly: "*What has become of the curiosities which Johnson collected* for Mrs Thrale's little girl?" What, indeed?—and at this time of day!—considering it is one hundred and twenty years ago.

Johnson once addressed a letter to a "Mr Tomkeson." The editor is much gravelled. "The name Tomkeson," he assures us, is not in Boswell? is not found in the parish lists? Nothing of the kind. "It is *not* in the indexes of the *Gentleman's Magazine*." That settles it. "There is no sich a person which his name is Tomkeson," as Mrs Gamp would say. As we know, a word not to be "found in Johnson's Dictionary" or in "the *Gentleman's Magazine*," fatally compromises it. "Perhaps the copyist has been at fault." Why not Johnson himself, who so often spelt phonetically? Tomkeson, Tompkinson, or Tomkinson are the same name, and the editor will find them in abundance in his *Gentleman's Magazine*.

Johnson finishes a letter with "To sleep, or not to sleep." Our careful editor, to make all clear, adds this explanation: "He is parodying 'Hamlet,' act iii., scene 1, line 56, 'To be, or not to be.'" On this one hardly knows what to say.

Johnson alluded to a "*parterre*." Every one surely knows what it means. We are told that "Johnson defines 'parterre' as a level of ground that faces the front of a house, and is generally finished with greens and flowers." The word "greens" then catching his eye, he must caution us. "Greens," he says gravely, "Johnson does not define *in its modern sense*, of a vegetable food," etc.

Dr B. Hill, who as we see is himself perpetually falling into mistakes, has, of course, an almost reverential tolerance for the most obvious misprints. Having to quote from Nichol's "Illustration," a passage in which it is said that "*Skakespeare* (*sic*) adopted all turns, etc," he is too scrupulous to make the change of a letter. And in one of his letters to Mrs Thrale, we find Johnson describing a visit to *Ham*, not the London suburb, but a well-known county seat in Derbyshire. We find that he took Boswell with him to *Ham*, . . . they went to *Ham*, etc. This, of course, was Mrs Piozzi's misreading for Islam, belonging to the Port family. The editor actually maintains the misprint, and the reader finds himself, in the text, taken to Ham, and to Ham again!

When one of her friends was sick, Johnson wrote to Mrs Thrale that "Physicians, be their powers less or more, are the only refuge we have." On which our ever-literal editor conceives that Johnson has now lost his faith. "*Johnson's piety here seems to slumber.*" He was, of course, only thinking of the comparative value of various earthly aids. As if the pious Johnson would, to restore Thrale to health, announce that there was no use in prayers.

Johnson described the arrival of Fathers Wilks and Brewer, English Benedictines from Paris, and the attentions he paid them. Says the editor: "Had they officiated as priests in England, if they were foreigners, the act was a felony; if natives, high treason." Dr B. Hill surely does not mean to convey that in 1776 the practice of the Catholic Faith was interdicted in England! Did not Mrs Thrale write to Johnson of the burning of chapels at Bath and Bristol, to say nothing of the London chapels, in which, of course, rites were celebrated?

When the editor comes to speak of the attempt that was made to obtain an increase of Johnson's pension, and which failed, in a sort of paroxysm of indignation he turns to an old Debrett's "Royal Kalendar for 1795," and there discovers that there were "twelve Lords of the Bedchamber," each receiving £1200 a year, and fourteen grooms of the Chamber, etc." No one can divine what is to come of this. The pensioned Johnson ought to have had one of these posts! "As Burns was made a gauger, *so Johnson might have been made a Lord, or at least a groom, of the Bedchamber.*" The notion of the poor old dying Johnson going about at court as "Lord Johnson"—or, better still, as "a groom of the Bedchamber"—is exquisitely funny. And as Burns was to be gratified with the humble office of a gauger, so Johnson was to be raised to the Peerage!

Johnson wrote that he had the honour of "saluting Flora Macdonald." The editor must explain. "By saluting, Johnson, *I believe meant kissing.*" I believe! Has he read old novels and old plays, or heard of "a chaste salute"? Nay, he even goes to look for it in the great Dictionary, where he assures us that Johnson actually gives it "as one of the meanings of the word."

In the month of November Johnson wrote to Mrs Thrale this simple observation, "You have at last begun to bathe." The subject of bathing, or the "*cold bath*," has always for the editor a fascination; and in other cases he has expended many laborious notes and quotations on the origin, etc., of bathing. Here he assures us gravely "*that the month of November is late in the year for bathing.*" Johnson was not thinking whether it was late or early, neither was Mrs Thrale; nor did it matter. She *had* bathed; that was certain. One may even traverse the editor's statement, and say that November is *not* late for bathing; it depends on the mildness of the season. But we are not yet done with this bathing matter. The editor is determined to *aprofondir* the whole. Johnson spoke of the "unaccountable terror a child has for some things"; particularly of "putting into the water a child who is well." I really don't know how to approach these things with due gravity, but here we have our commentator earnestly assuring us that by "putting into the water" was meant "putting into the sea—*for they were at Brighton.*"

Among numerous other startling things, we are told that Johnson did not know how to spell, that in our day spelling is a "mean" thing; that too much is thought of it. "It will *bring comfort, methinks*, to those who are ignorant to know that Johnson was as ignorant." I say nothing of these persons; but as to Johnson, he is altogether astray. Johnson spelt correctly, according to the standard of his day, but there were many words whose spelling was not fixed. "Gaiety" was sometimes "gayety." "Boswell" Johnson always spelt with one *l*, "harass" with two *r*'s, and *k* was often added to "public" and such words. Who would think of calling such variations bad spelling?

Johnson, as we have seen, spelt "Boswell" with one *l*, and "Scott" with one *t*. This was almost a habit with him. On this spelling of "Scott" Dr B. Hill is perfectly astounding: "He *was perhaps paying to the future Lord Stowell a delicate compliment*." An odd fashion of complimenting, this, by docking one letter! But it was in this way: Lord Eldon, it seems, once sat next a gentleman who told him that he spelt *his* name "Scot," as being more distinguished. And *therefore* Johnson, perhaps, "intended a delicate compliment." And observe, Lord Eldon records it as an oddity, not as a compliment. Johnson, of course, "intended" nothing at all—spelling the word by a sort of instinct. It may be, however, that Dr B. Hill intends something facetious.

Johnson wrote proposing to go to Birmingham and Oxford. "And there (at Oxford) we will have a row, and a dinner, and a dish of tea." This seems plain. "But," says the editor, "*I do not understand what this means.*" What does a *row* signify? Flying to the great Dictionary, he finds "row" explained as—what think you?—"A file, a rank, a number of things ranged in line." Johnson does not recognise the sense of "an excursion in a rowing boat." But he *has* the verb "to row," to take excursions in a rowing boat; and there are many illustrations given. Yet "I do not understand what this means." Neither "is it likely that in his weak health he would go on the river so late." Very probable; but Johnson was merely talking and planning, and possibly did *not* go on the river.

Johnson wrote to Garrick, in reference to their deceased friend, Dr Hawkesworth, that he had no letters of the latter. The editor tells us that there is a letter to Garrick from one Wray, who says he will leave to Goldsmith's friends the task of honouring his memory. From these two scraps the editor gravely concludes: "*It is possible* that Garrick planned memoirs of Goldsmith and Hawkesworth"! The idea of Garrick as a memoir-writer is rather novel. Further on, he tells us that the edition of Hawkesworth's life and writings was being actually prepared by Ryland. Garrick had merely asked Johnson for letters. As to the Goldsmith theory, the editor demolishes it for us himself, for he says timorously: "Perhaps Wray refers only to Goldsmith's monument in Westminster Abbey"! So he does.

There is a "Caled" Harding mentioned: "A misprint, *I conjecture*, for Caleb." But why not apply to his faithful and oft-consulted *Gentle-*

man's Magazine? There *I* found it, "Caleb Harding, Mansfield, Notts, Physician"—and without any conjecturing.

But here is a strange surmise. When Mrs Thrale was christening one of her daughters, Johnson wrote: "You must let us have a Bessy another time." "No doubt Johnson had asked *that one of Thrale's daughters should bear the name of his wife*"*!* As if he would speak in this jocular way of his loved "Tetty," or thrust her name on a family who knew nothing of her! He surely meant that it was a good old English name, or a family name.

In some trifling points Dr B. Hill's blindness is perfectly confounding. Johnson wrote to Mrs Thrale from the country of the high price of malt, that little profit was made: "But there is often a *rise upon stock*. Some in the town have made £50 by the *rise upon stock*," *i.e.* the funds. But hearken to our editor: "Johnson refers, *I suppose*, to the rise in the value of the stock *of malt*"(!) With due caution he adds: "He *may* be speaking of the funds." "May"! And then, to demolish his own theory, he quotes the prices of the year, showing a rise of *ten* pounds in the funds!

Once Johnson, returning to town, took boat at Gravesend, and landed at Billingsgate, whence he had to walk some distance before he found a coach. The editor is much dissatisfied at this arrangement. He finds out that a bell was rung at Gravesend at high tide by night and day. "*Surely* the bell was rung at low tide," Dr B. Hill says piteously, "so that the boat might be carried up by the flow." We cannot tell anything about this bell. The rule applied to, we are assured, "tilt boats" also—that is, boats with sails as well as to wherries—and the bell rang at Billingsgate also, where the high tide would suit the voyage to Gravesend. In any case, the ringing of the bell or the tide had nothing to do with Johnson. Then, Johnson, in his honest way, says, when he landed, he had to carry his budget to Cornhill before he got a coach. But the editor, not quite satisfied with this, could have told him what to do: "*From Billingsgate the most convenient way for Johnson would have been to take a sculling-boat to Temple Stairs.*" Still, he can make allowance for Johnson's behaviour on this occasion. He knew what was in his mind. "*Doubtless* the state of the tide made it dangerous *to pass under London Bridge*." There is no evidence of this. The truth was, Billingsgate was the end of the journey. Johnson, "I conjecture," had had enough of the water, and a coach would cost him but little more. Well, he carried his "budget" part of the way. Budget? thinks our editor, what is this? "Johnson defines it as a bag easily carried." And then, to prevent mistakes of careless people who might fancy Johnson was helping the Exchequer in some way by "*carrying his Budget*," we are assured "that the sense in which it is commonly used, of the yearly financial statement of the Chancellor of the Exchequer, is *not given in the Dictionary.*"

"Of this parcel," wrote Johnson of some MS. submitted to him, "I have rejected no poetry." Is it not plain, and Johnsonian, too? But the editor must oddly amend, and puts "ejected": "Of this parcel I have *ejected* no poetry." To see Johnson ejecting poetry from parcels must have been a rare sight.

But here is a very elaborate blunder. Johnson wrote jocosely of a day "that you never saw before, as Doodle says," etc. Now, who was Doodle? The editor makes diligent research, and finds out that Doodle was a character in one of Ravenscroft's plays, called "The London Cuckolds," and in which Doodle figured as an alderman. This is very precise. We have then some interesting details as to this play—how it was always performed at a particular season, and how, later, Garrick, in the interests of decency and morals, had abolished the performance, and substituted "George Barnwell" for the old piece. This was all so particular that, though having my own view on the matter, I was staggered, and took down the play to look out the words which Johnson had quoted, and "Alderman Doodle" was presumed to have uttered. To my surprise they were not there. Most people know that they belong to a much better known play—"Tom Thumb"—where are the two burlesque lords, "Noodle and Doodle," who open the piece with a song, in which are the words quoted by Johnson. It is clear that the editor could not have taken the trouble to look for the lines.

Next for a strange "jumble." Johnson spoke of some friends, whose names are suppressed by Mrs Thrale, and represented by the initials C, B, and D. These admittedly refer to Fanny Burney, Cumberland, and Dr Delap. Presently we find Johnson alluding to a friend as one * * * who had lost £20,000 in a speculation, adding, "Neither D nor B has given occasion to *his* loss." This loser is later spoken of as C. The editor at once leaps to the conclusion that C must be Cumberland, especially as D and B —that is, Fanny Burney and her friend Delap —"fit in," as he calls it. Let us see how they "fit in." Johnson tells us: "Of B (Fanny), I suppose the fact is true that *he* is gone; but, for *his* loss, who can tell who has been the winner?" *His* loss, mark! So our editor asks us to believe that the struggling Cumberland had lost £20,000; that "Fanny" had been "plunging," and had fled the country! All which is ludicrous.

It might be, indeed, that there is hardly a single "discovery," "conjecture," or "theory," of the editor's that does not break down in some way. Thus, we have a letter of Johnson's to Lowe, the painter, which the editor arbitrarily dates May 15th, 1778. Johnson writes to him that he had mentioned his case to Reynolds and Garrick, but that both were "cold." Garrick, however, seemed to relent: "I think you have reason to expect something from him. But he must be tenderly handled. I have just, however, received what will please and gratify you. I have sent it just as it came." This, the editor fancies, refers to a letter from Garrick, in which Lowe gratefully acknowledges a gift of ten pounds from the actor, sent on May 15th, 1778. "*It was very likely that sum which Johnson sent on just as it came.*" It will be seen in a moment, as the editor ought to have seen, that this will not hold, for had not Johnson told Lowe plainly that Garrick was "cold"; that he must be handled tenderly; that nothing at the moment was to be got from him? "*However*," he adds, "I send you something that will please you," etc. Not surely from Garrick, for Johnson would have said, "but he has just sent me ten pounds for you"—but some encouraging letter or promise from some one else. This is the meaning of this "However"—that is, "though we have failed with Garrick for the present, I send you something else that will console you."

"Save one's hay," getting one's hay "saved," are familiar phrases enough even to non-farmers. Johnson had written that if the weather continued fine, "it will certainly save hay. But that would not make up for the scanty harvest." Nothing could be clearer or more commonplace; but, to our utter bewilderment, we are gravely assured that the fine weather would save the hay, "by *making the grass grow*, *so that there would be food for the cattle.*" A fresh crop was miraculously to come up under a spell of fine weather, and thus the farmer would be *saved* using his hay! What are we to think?

Describing a wager between Macbean and one Hamilton, as to the date when the Dictionary would be completed, the editor strangely announces that this Hamilton "had some share in the printing of the Dictionary," though he concedes that "a great deal of it was done by Strahan." Anything more unwarranted or far-fetched could not be conceived. Every Johnsonian knows that Strahan was the printer of the Dictionary, and a printer of importance, who had no need of any extra aid. Such a thing was unheard of. And on the title we read: "Printed by W. Strahan." The book took some years going through the press, and each sheet was worked off as it was ready, and the type distributed, so there was no strain on the establishment. And after all, the editor is not sure that this Hamilton *was* Hamilton the printer. "Hamilton *was likely* Archibald Hamilton, the printer."

A touch will cause the editor's most ingenious speculations to topple over in the most curious way. Thus, when on the eve of his quarrel with Mr Thrale, Johnson complained that "Susy had not written, and *Miss Thrale* had sent him only one letter," the editor detects here an early symptom of coldness. *Miss* Thrale, mark! "He does not call her Queeney." Still he called the other girl "Susy," and turning over a few pages we find him calling her "Queeney," or "Queenie," just as usual!

Here is one of the editor's odd speculations—too unsound, of course. Johnson, when at Oxford, went with his host, Dr Edwards, to see his living, which was only five miles off. "*No doubt*," the editor says gravely, "*they returned the same day*." We neither doubt nor assent; we cannot tell; nor does it matter. In default of all knowledge of details of the visit, the editor sets his imagination to work, and taking down his Lewis's "Topographical Dictionary," finds out that "the old Manor House, which had belonged to Speaker Lenthal, was still standing." Something could be got out of this. We are asked to picture Johnson going over the rooms. "*No doubt*"—yes, but there *is* doubt—"he was *gravely* told a story about Cromwell's visit, and how he concealed himself, and was let down in a chair," etc. Gravely told! The editor almost fancies that he was by.

Johnson wrote that, as he lived among the various orders of mankind, he was familiar with "the exploits, sometimes of the philosophers, sometimes of the pickpockets." This is plain enough; but the editor illustrates it by this mysterious, oracular utterance, "*The two orders sometimes met*." This has no bearing on Johnson's remark. Of course, all classes of society may, and do "meet"—in the streets, at public places, etc. But it turns out that the editor intends to be jocose, for it seems that when a balloon was going up some noblemen and gentlemen lost their watches and purses, and in this way "*the two orders sometimes met*." But even this is inaccurate. For here the two orders did *not* meet; Johnson was speaking of the "philosophers and pickpockets"; these were "noblemen and gentlemen."

Whenever *weather* of any kind is mentioned—be it fine or bad, "rain or shine"—our editor is certain to start off on a course of minute meteorological investigations, tracing out not only what was the weather of the moment, but what was it before, and what was it after. It is hard to deal with these things in sober seriousness; so genuine, indeed, is Dr B. Hill in his enthusiasm that he is quite unconscious of the absurdity. Thus, at the end of August, 1777, Johnson wrote this casual remark from the country: "The weather was *à merveille*." Then Dr B. Hill starts off on his eccentric enquiries, and discovers that "the earlier part of the summer *had been very wet*," which did not matter, as Johnson was dealing with the latter portion. Our old friend Walpole is then introduced to confirm this general "wetness," though it has to be admitted that by the end of September, more than a month after Johnson wrote, "all was lustre and brilliancy." This is likely enough; for we may conclude, cheerfully, that at one time it may have been fine and at another wet. Still he is troubled by the thought that Johnson had stated that about the middle of September "we have at last fine weather—in Derbyshire"; but we are reassured by the news that "the weather in Staffordshire had been extraordinarily fine nearly three weeks earlier." This is an odd mania, and we really do not know what to make of it. It suggests a comic character in "Money," who is always remarking that it is "seasonable weather"!

Writing to India, Johnson said piously, and picturesquely, too: "Prayers can pass the line and tropics." The editor cannot resist having his "little joke" here: "Prayers would, *apparently*, take the longer course round the Cape of Good Hope." This alone would show little *feeling* by Dr B. Hill for the duty he has undertaken.

Walpole described Dr Birch as "running about in quest of anything new or old." On which the editor: "*He ran about in more senses than one*, for he walked round London." How could he run about if he "walked"? The truth was, Dr Birch made an interesting peregrination round London, and this was not "running about in more senses than one," or in any sense. Walpole's meaning was figurative. Dr Birch was an ardent antiquary, who, like Boswell, hunted for information everywhere; but he did not actually "run" as he enquired.

The editor has an odd *phobia* as to applying the term "girl" to any one over twenty. He will not have it. Johnson wrote affectionately to his "Tetty": "Now, my dear girl." The editor objects that "she was past forty or fifty." On another occasion Johnson called Hannah More "a saucy girl." Again the editor interposes: "She was between thirty and forty." Surely he must have heard of "an old girl." But this is sheer trifling. As we saw, he will not have "boy" either.

And again: "Did you stay all night at Sir J. Reynolds's," wrote Johnson to Mrs Thrale, "and keep Miss up again?" Any one would understand this. But the editor supplies this comment: "Miss, who was kept up again, *was Miss Thrale*." And if we are to be so minute, why alter the sense? Miss was *not* kept up; Johnson merely enquired if she had been.

Once on the tour Johnson described how there were no seats for the ladies in the boat, or, as he put it, "accommodations." This the editor explains in a rather amusing way. "Johnson commonly says accommodations where we should say 'conveniences.'" Where has Dr B. Hill been living all this time? Should we, or *do* we, say this? On a boating party at Oxford, for instance, would one of the young oarsmen announce that there were no "*conveniences* for the ladies." For this word "accommodation," the editor seems to have an odd fancy. In another place, we find him lingering fondly over it, and quoting "who do not obstruct accommodation," etc., which he explains as "provision of consideration," with much more.

He sometimes makes wild conjectures—apparently for the reason that he thinks the thing *ought* to be so. Thus we are told: "It is probable that Mrs Cobb and Mrs Adey, with their brother, were joint owners of Edial Hall when Johnson took it for an academy." There is not the faintest ground for this assertion. Dr B. Hill must know that it is no more "probable" that it belonged to these people than that it belonged to the Garricks or to Walmesley, or to any one else in Lichfield.

Surely every one knows that the "gear" of a horse means a part of his harness. But the editor gravely assures us that "in Johnson's Dictionary gears signifies 'the traces by which horses *or oxen* draw,'" etc.

When Johnson speaks of consulting the "Edinburgh Dispensatory," the editor tells us that "in the *Gentleman's Magazine* of 1747 is advertised the 'Edinburgh Pharmacopœia,' edited by W. Lewis," assuming that this was the work Johnson consulted. Nothing of the kind. It was, as Johnson knew, and accurately stated, the "Edinburgh Dispensatory," a well-known medical work published in 1733, and of which there are several editions.

It is often almost incomprehensible how Dr B. Hill can so mistake the meaning of his text. Johnson wrote "of the petticoat government he had never heard," and of some Shakespeare discovery, that "no one had seen the wonders." To explain the first of these recondite allusions, the editor refers us to other passages: "I am miserable under petticoat government," and, "See how I live when I am not under petticoat government." But is it not plain that he was alluding to some story about a friend supposed to be suffering from female tyranny? The editor adds a more amazing hypothesis: "It is possible that some *political pamphlet* had been brought out under that title in imitation of one by Dunton in 1702." As if people could recall a pamphlet nearly eighty years old.

And what was the Dramatic Discovery? According to our editor, these "wonders," of which Johnson knew nothing, this dramatic curiosity of which he was only "told," was neither more nor less than a *new book* written by Johnson himself!—a supplement to his Shakespeare in two volumes—his own book: a discovery of which the author was *once* told by Miss Lawrence. But it would be foolish to go further with the matter. Johnson was clearly speaking of some portrait, or play, or fabrication that had just come to light.

Johnson wrote to his dying mother that he did not think her "unfit to face death," which leads the editor into this rhapsody: "How Johnson's *truthfulness* stands forth here! Not flattering at that dread hour . . . it is all that he *dared* say even to his mother." Considering that the poor old lady was *ninety* years old, anything in the way of "flattering" her, *i.e.* holding out delusive hopes of living, was not likely to occur to her son or to herself. But, as it was, Johnson, in the tenderest way, *did* encourage her to live: "Endeavour to do all you can for yourself. *Eat as much as you can*," etc. Even the grand "truthfulness" which stood forth at "that dread hour" did not amount to saying, "You cannot live," but that he thought she was well prepared if she should die. What Dr B. Hill means, after so extolling Johnson for his blunt truthfulness, by saying "it is all he dared to say even to his mother," I cannot divine. The editor then announces, *en passant*, "Travelling was then very slow." In proof of which we are told of a certain nobleman who, travelling in his coach and six, took two whole days to go ninety miles. Who was this nobleman? He is not found in the "Peerage"; he and his coach and six exist only in "Tom Jones"! And good going it was, considering; for, having six horses, it was probably a heavy Berline. But Johnson could have taken the ordinary night coach.

Here is another strange misconception. Johnson wrote to Mrs Thrale: "To-day I went to look into my places in the Borough." Johnson, as we know, often associated himself with the brewery, speaking of it as "ours"—"*we* shall brew," etc. Looking into "my places" surely meant something of this kind. The editor tells us it was "his room," or, rather, the "receptacles in it in the Thrales' house in the Borough." But "places" is never used in this sense, as cabinets or drawers, etc. We never heard that Johnson lived with the Thrales at the Borough, or that he had a room there, or kept his things there, though he had a room at Streatham. The common-sense meaning surely is that he went round to look at "my places in the Borough" — the brewhouse, etc., to see and report how things were going on. Further, once writing from Oxford he tells how he showed some one "the places." He adds, as if to explain, "I called on Mr Perkins in the counting-house," another of his "places."

Johnson wrote to one Hollyer, who, according to Mr Croker, was his cousin. The editor doubts this. "The tone of his letter is not that of one who is writing to his first cousin." Now, here Johnson speaks of his relation Thomas Johnson, whom he calls "*our* cousin," that is, cousin to both Hollyer and Johnson; and he describes him as a "man almost equally related to both of us." Could anything be clearer?

Dr Burney, it seems, went to Oxford to study in the libraries, on which important point our editor, like his hero Jamie, "gangs clean daft." First, he notes the strange circumstance that it was the only week in the year in which the library was shut up. This "shutting up" becomes a very serious matter, though it does not affect Johnson or Boswell in any way. At this time "the inspection was held once a year"; but we must note that "a custom had apparently arisen of closing the library a week beforehand for the sake of getting ready," etc. Even this information is rather speculative, for we are told that the custom had only *apparently* arisen. Still, we must get on as well as we can. It is much to know that this custom of "*closing for cleaning*" was actually sanctioned by the statutes of 1813. With such praiseworthy thoroughness does our editor trace all about this "closing for cleaning" that he discovers that it is *now* closed during the first week of October. And then, what fee did Dr Burney *pay?* Here, again, the editor gets no further than an "apparently." "Apparently the fees were the same at the time of Dr Burney's visit." And next, who was librarian at the time of Dr Burney's visit? Why, the Rev. J. Price. Then we ramble off to Dr Beddoes, the reader in chemistry, who was accused of having lent a copy of Cook's "Voyages." And all this hotchpot about Dr Burney having gone to the Bodleian!

Johnson wrote to Taylor these simple words: "I am moved; I fancy I shall move again." The editor is much struck with the word "moved," and begs our attention to this strange peculiarity: "Johnson, writing the word at the end of one line and at the beginning of the next, divides it '*mo-ved.*'" *C'est immense!*

If there is any one whom Dr B. Hill strives to lessen, or even to degrade, it is, perhaps, Johnson himself. He is constantly trying to show that he is inconsistent, unfeeling, etc. In this connection it is astonishing to find him charging Johnson with sanctioning bribery and corruption at elections! When Thrale lost his seat Johnson tried to find another for him.

"As seats," he wrote, "are to be had *without natural interest*," he fancied persons might be found "who transact such affairs." This is twisted into corruptly purchasing a seat! And Johnson, moreover, was falsifying his principles, for he had written elsewhere: "The statutes against bribery were intended to prevent upstarts with money from getting into Parliament." I should be ashamed to defend Johnson against such accusations. The meaning of his words was that there were seats open to persons "without natural interest"; that is, who were unconnected with the place. These were patronage boroughs, and boroughs which might be glad to have a wealthy citizen like Thrale. He, moreover, was not an "upstart" with money to whom the statutes would apply. He had been in Parliament, and was well known. The whole is absurd.

On the death of Mrs Thrale's son Johnson wrote a letter of condolence. "Poor Ralph is gone." She had done her best to save him. The boy had not suffered much. "Think on those who are left to you." He then passes on to other topics. Surely this seems feeling enough, and sympathetic too. But not enough for our editor. It is "a strange letter." He attacks his hero for being so heartless. "The childless Johnson was ignorant of the feelings of a parent." But I refer the editor to Johnson's truly affectionate and condoling letters on the deaths of the other children (March 25 and 30, 1776), and let him say if Johnson was ignorant of the feelings of a parent.

Johnson also wrote to her to say that he had declined a ball and supper. His editor "has him" here, and wishes to prove him insincere. "*He had, however*, attended the Lichfield Theatre on the day on which the news arrived of the boy's death." This criticism, again, shows how little the editor understands human nature and the course of human actions. To go to a local theatre in a country town, and where his relations to the Thrales, and the death itself, were almost unknown, was a different thing from going to a ball and supper in London, where it would seem unbecoming. This is too elementary for discussion.

"I wish Ralph better," wrote Johnson on another occasion to Mrs Thrale of her son, and my master (Mr Thrale) and his boys well." Could any statement be put in plainer language? —Ralph was one boy, Harry the other. He wished Ralph better, and Mr Thrale and his sons happiness. Yet thus the editor: "*Who he meant by his boys I do not know.*"

The editor again, eager to catch Johnson tripping, points out that he had spelt a Mr Kindersley's name wrongly as "Kinsderley." It is amusing to find the corrector himself falling into a blunder of the same kind in the very act of correction, for he points out that it should be "Kinsdersley." The bewildered reader is thus told that Johnson is wrong, and is asked to substitute what is also wrong. Not content with this, he tries to set Johnson right on another point, and with equal success. Johnson spoke of a book, written by this Mr Kindersley, and the editor announces that it was by *Mrs* Kindersley. But on reading the passage carefully and quietly, as Dr B. Hill should have done, we find Johnson saying, "Mr Kindersley and *another lady*"—which clearly shows that he had written Mrs Kindersley, and that the printer or Mrs Thrale had misread him.

Johnson wrote: "At Lichfield, my native place, I hope to show a good example by frequent attendance at church." Most natural, and most plain too. He lays out his plan, and gives his reason for it, viz. "to show a good example." But the editor sees something below. Recalling how Johnson once stood in the market-place, to expiate his unfilial conduct, he gravely tells us that he here wished to do an act of "penance"! This is incredible, but so it is. It seems that over sixty years before, when Johnson was a boy, "*he had played truant from church*," and by going to church now, he would make atonement before his fellow-citizens! As if the act would have this effect on the Lichfield folk! As if they could remember that a little boy "had played truant from church"! and above all, as if Johnson would think his regular duty of going to church was an act of penance!

Johnson's house in Lichfield was close to Sadler Street, and he once alluded pleasantly to what he calls "the revolutions of Sadler Street." We cannot tell what these were, but the editor knows. They were certainly changes in the local force of watchmen. Cue for the orchestra! Did not these watchmen carry "Bills"? and did not the editor during "my visit to Lichfield" see these actual "Bills." Then we have Shakespeare's Dogberry introduced; and it was curious that Dogberry's men also had "Bills." They were also carried in "the Court of Array," which leads on to "the Statutes of Array." We are then taken—by heaven knows what concatenation!—to the city gaol, which was in a bad state; and then, as might be expected, to John Howard. But the editor cannot shake himself clear of the Watch, and so we return to them. It seems they used to be called "dozeners." That word sends us off to the Isle of Man, where it seems there are "vintiners." Each "vintiner" had a *vintaine*, etc. Poor Johnson!

Johnson spoke of a gentleman who had erected a commemoratory urn to him, and which he said was like burying him in his lifetime. Dr B. Hill says that Boswell mentions a Colonel Myddleton, of Wales, who had done this, but adds that he could not be the person Johnson spoke of, as the inscription showed that it was put up after Johnson's death. This is quite wrong. Boswell is speaking of "the abundant homage paid to Johnson *during his life*," and gives this Myddleton urn as an instance, with its inscription: "This spot was often dignified by the presence of, etc., whose moral writings, etc., give ardour to virtue," etc. That this was the gentleman referred to by Johnson, seems all but certain, as it is unlikely that there would be *two* persons who erected urns. Further, Johnson heard it through Mrs Thrale, who was a Welsh woman, and Colonel Myddleton was Welsh also, and actually writes that it was being done, and that it was like burying him alive.

Johnson wrote of his old friend Mrs Aston, "as being, I fancy, about sixty-eight. Is it likely that she will ever be better?" Here the editor, seeing into Johnson's mind, assures us that "*he was thinking of himself, for* sixty-eight was his own age." How unsophisticated is Dr B. Hill, and how little does he know of old people in general, and of Johnson in particular! As if the latter would fancy that Mrs Aston's case could apply to *him*. He was always thinking, on the contrary, that he *would* get better, and he would shut out the notion of their both being of the same age; or, if he *did* think it, he would, perhaps, lay the flattering unction to himself that he was the same age, but in vigour much younger.

Mrs Thrale mentions a visit from a "Mr R——" who, she thought, "would drive her wild." The editor opines that "he was some schemer or projector, with designs on Mrs Thrale's purse." There is nothing to show that the man was a schemer, or projector, or wanted to get at Mrs Thrale's purse. So blinded is the editor by his delusions, that he cannot see that only a few lines above Johnson tells all about him. Mr R—— simply wanted a place! He had skill in keeping accounts, and he wished to have Perkins' office. Johnson thought it was better to keep Perkins. And out of this the editor engenders the theory that he wanted to rob or swindle Mrs Thrale!

The editor notes how in his money difficulties Johnson "never turned to Garrick." He adds in a bewildering way: "Reynolds, moreover, was in great prosperity, *for* he had in 1758 150 letters." What is the connection, particularly in that "moreover"? So with the odd proof of great prosperity—"*for* he had 150 letters." Equally mysterious is how it all proves that Johnson "never turned to Garrick in his distresses."

Johnson, speaking of a chapel in which were some gravestones, said: "Without some of the ancient families . . . still continued their sepulture." Who could fail to understand this? Some people buried in the chapel, but the more ancient families preferred the churchyard. But no: "What Johnson means by 'without' in this passage at first sight *is not clear*."

He himself will strive to make clearer the clearest statements. Thus Johnson wrote: "Boswell wishes to draw me to Lichfield, and, as I love to travel with him, I have a mind to be drawn." But this must be obscure to readers, the editor thinks, so it is explained to us: "Boswell, who was returning to Scotland, *no doubt*, wished Johnson to accompany him as far as Lichfield." No doubt he did. Again, when Johnson says, as plainly as he can, that some one "had offered Perkins money, but that it was not wanted," the editor obligingly tells us that the person in question "had offered, *no doubt*, to advance money to Perkins, if any were needed." These are wonderful "no doubts."

Where "Mr C." is mentioned, the editor, speculating whether it be Mr Crutchley or Mr Cator that is intended, always contrives to mistake. Johnson states that a "Mr C." had offered Perkins money, but that it was not wanted. The editor assures us that Cator, who was one of the executors, "had offered, *no doubt*, to advance money to Perkins, but it was not wanted." Why repeat this bit of information which we had already? But it was surely *not* Cator, as the editor ought to know, for he presently quotes Miss Burney, who says that *Mr Crutchley* offered to lend Perkins £1000.

As the editor takes Cator for Crutchley where Crutchley was meant, so he takes Crutchley for Cator where Cator was intended.

Johnson had said: "If he goes to ——, he will be overpowered with words as good as his own." This talker, the editor announces, was Mr Crutchley, who was one of the trustees. But Johnson had just complained of another of the trustees, Mr Cator, who, he said, "speaks with great exuberance." This was surely the person Johnson referred to. He sees this Cator everywhere. Thus, when some successful and retired tradesman complained that he had no power of talk—"I go to conversations, but I have no conversation"—this was, of course, Cator, according to the editor. But, as we have just seen, Cator "speaks with great exuberance." He was a great talker; as Miss Burney says, "gives his opinion upon everything." The truth was, Cator was a man of weight, culture, an M.P., a person of large fortune, a squire, and, certainly not "a retired tradesman."

As to Dr Collier's epitaph, Johnson writes: "You may set S—— S—— at defiance." "The S—— S——," thus the editor objects, "she (Mrs Piozzi) says means 'Streatfield,' forgetful of the final 's,'" a trivial point at most. But the lady was perfectly right. "S—— S——" were the initials of the "nick-name" of the well-known "Sophy Streatfield," for whom Dr Collier has such an attachment, and who figures in Miss Burney's Diary. It was two names, not one.

Dr B. Hill affects a sort of sagacity in "discovering" that a certain letter, without any address, was written to Lord Shelburne; but the letter itself reveals the name as plainly as if it were written on it. Johnson distinguishes between mother and wife—"with Lady Shelburne I once had the honour," etc.; "to *your lady* I am a stranger," etc. Plain as a pikestaff.

The strange confusion into which his wild

guesses lead the editor is well shown by the following: "Mr ——— was not calamity," wrote Johnson in June 1783, "it was his sister. I am afraid the term is now strictly applicable, for she seems to have fallen some way into obscurity, I am afraid, by a palsy," etc. To explain which, the editor refers us, "see *post*," to a letter of about a fortnight later, in which Johnson wrote: "Your Bath news shows me new calamities. I am told Mrs L—— is left with a numerous family, very slenderly supplied." This, according to Dr B. Hill, was the "calamity" referred to before. But Johnson says "*new* calamities," *i.e.* one in addition to the other which was an old one. This Mrs L—— was Mrs Lewis, the wife of the Dean of Ossory. Her "calamity" was being left in poverty; in the first case, the calamity was a palsy. They were distinct persons. But, beguiled by his theory, the editor goes on to entangle himself still more. Johnson later had recurred to the first case; he was glad she was not left in poverty; her *disease* was sufficient misery. Again the editor notes, "probably Mrs L—— (the Dean's wife) mentioned *ante*." Johnson, a year later, speaks of this palsied lady as not being well. Only at this stage the editor thought of looking up the date of the Dean's death, which he found took place before June 8; that is, before the allusion to the first calamity. So the whole fabric tumbles down. In this awkward position he tries to rescue himself by having recourse to his usual device—the letters were wrongly placed! And he tries to supply a new and proper date by a fresh theory equally unfounded. Johnson on June 5 spoke of Mrs Thrale's pity for "a thief that had made the gallows idle." He was sorry for his suicide, but "I suppose he would have gone to the gallows,' etc. This surely refers to some common malefactor. But no; he means an eminent contractor, one Powell, who had made free with the public monies and committed suicide. But we need not consider the matter further, for the editor himself tells us that his solution "was possible, though not probable," and finally adds, "it does not seem likely *that he would have been tried on the capital* charge."

Johnson wrote that their daily fare at Ashbourne was "*Toujours* strawberries and cream." The editor assures us that Johnson was quoting or adapting the French proverb, "*Toujours perdrix*." That proverb is always quoted to *illustrate* some monotonous repetitions of the same person, story, song, or fare; but Johnson was merely stating the literal fact that there was "always strawberries and cream." More amazing is the further illustration of this trivial point by a quotation from Swift on a poet, who, he says, may ring changes in rhymes and words, "*but the reader generally finds it all pork*." Johnson has strawberries and cream every day, and so resembles a poet whose rhymes suggest pork, etc. What does it mean?

Johnson disapproved of the Royal Marriage Act because "he would not have the people think that its validity depended on the will of a man." This passage, we are told, "puzzled Mr Croker and Mr Lockhart"; why, it would be hard to say, for nothing could be more intelligible. He consulted his *Gentleman's Magazine*, the following extract from which "throws light on Johnson's meaning." The Bill would help the King to change the order of succession, for, by putting his veto on the proposed marriage of his eldest son, he could thus "*bring in the younger son*." All which is sheer delusion, and a mare's nest, and poor Johnson is made to talk utter nonsense. He was, of course, not thinking of such things, but of the religious question. Marriage was the function of the Church, and indissoluble, and not to depend on the will of a man. When Johnson said "no man can run away from himself," he was thinking, we are told, of the familiar quotation, "*cœlum non animum*," etc. Every scholar will supply the true line, which is even more hackneyed, "Patriœ quis exul se quoque fugit."

When Johnson writes to Mrs Thrale of the polling at Oxford, the editor supplies us with a long analysis of the voters, and finally tells us that "*only fourteen* had *two Christian names; not quite one in thirty-five*." Is childish too strong a word for this sort of "information"?

There is a delightful "characteristical" note on "Mussels and Whilks." Johnson on one occasion writes that "I saw mussels and whilks." Most people would know *what* these words meant. But we must go far deeper. "Johnson *only* gives this word (whilk) *incidentally* in his Dictionary." Wise Johnson! The next best thing is to look out the word *welk*, under "to welk." Our editor tells us "Whilk is used for a small shell-fish." Further, whelk Johnson defines as (1), an inequality, a protuberance; (2), a pustule, and so on.

The editor has, as he fancies, discovered two blunders of the late Mr John Forster's, in his popular "Life of Goldsmith." Knowing how this admirable critic and correct writer was distinguished for accuracy and knowledge of his subject, I was certain—before examination even—that these charges would prove unfounded. And so it turned out. There was one Cooke, a friend of Goldsmith's, whom Mr Forster described as a young Irish law student, living near Goldsmith in the Temple. Now, as Goldsmith, the editor tells us, did not reside in the Temple till 1763, and as Cooke was old enough to have published his "Hesiod" in 1728, and to have found a place in the "Dunciad," poor foolish Mr Forster must have been quite astray in his facts. But the editor has confounded an English Thomas Cooke, who lived near the beginning of the century, with a William Cooke of Cork, who was alive in 1820—a personage that Dr B. Hill ought to have heard of. This is a serious blunder. He then deals with Mr Forster's other mistake, of confusing "Moore the Fabulist," better known as the writer of "The Gamester," with Dr Moore, the author of "Zeluco." Well, we turn to the text of "The Life," and find, to our astonishment, that Mr Forster was speaking of *Edward* Moore (who was the "fabulist"), and *not* of Dr John Moore of "Zeluco" fame. So there could be no possible foundation for this rather wanton charge; but I at last discovered that in the *Index* Moore was described as the author of "Zeluco." Mr Forster, as I learned from himself, did not prepare his own indexes, and I recollect his telling me he was not satisfied with the index to "The Life." The author is fairly only accountable for his text. Of course, had he, like Dr B. Hill, prepared his own monumental index, a volume strong, he would be chargeable.

When the Hebridean Tourists were proceeding from Montrose to Laurencekirk, they crossed a certain bridge. They little dreamed what a mysterious incident was occurring close by. The editor's note is so astonishing that I must give it in full. He begins: "James Mill was born on April the 6th, 1773, at Northwater Bridge, Parish of Logie, Pert, Forfar. The bridge was on the great central line of communication from the North of Scotland. *The hamlet is right and left of the road. Bain's* 'Life of Mill,' p. 1. Boswell and Johnson, on the road to Laurencekirk, must have passed by close to the cottage *in which he was lying, a baby not five months old*." Observe, not even John Stuart Mill, but the more obscure James. Nor is there even a certainty that he was "lying there a baby." And what had it all to do with

Johnson or Boswell, who in their lives must have passed numbers of places where more or less obscure people were "lying as babies?"

Surveying the ruins at St Andrews, Johnson pronounced that it was "a sorrowful scene," and very naturally, for these were devastated churches. The editor tells us: "One sorrowful scene Johnson was *perhaps too late* in the year to see." And what was this?—a death?—illness? Why, nothing but some broken windows in one of the colleges!

There is a critical instinct that comes of familiarity with turns of thought and character, and which almost infallibly guides us to the meaning. "Davies," Johnson wrote, "has had great success as an author, generated by the corruption of a bookseller," a pleasant sarcasm, which is surely intelligible. He means that the success of the authorship was owing to the knowledge of the "tricks of the trade," or that the authorship was of the inferior sort that might be expected from a crafty bookseller. The editor can see nothing of this. Johnson intended to point at Davies having been *a bankrupt! There* was "the corruption of the bookseller." With this interpretation Johnson's saying becomes unmeaning, for there is no corruption in bankruptcy as regards authorship. Moreover, Davies's bankruptcy had occurred some years before.

Johnson wrote to his friend Taylor that a Dr Wilson "can have no money," etc. Here is a specimen of the fashion in which Dr B. Hill will mistake the *plain* meaning of a passage. "Taylor," he says, "might have had some dispute" with Wilson. But the passage is clear—Wilson had a dispute, not with Taylor, but with a "Mr B." Johnson writes that the case is clear on Mr B.'s side, and Taylor intervening had merely drawn up some paper to help his friend, which Johnson praised. The editor tells us also, in reference to Taylor's quarrel with his wife: "Boswell seems to have known nothing of this matter." What! Boswell, who went on visits to Taylor with Johnson, who talked over his affairs with Johnson, and who was inquisitive enough—would he not have asked about Taylor's wife? As Taylor was alive, and helped him in his work, he was naturally silent on this delicate point.

When comforting Mrs Thrale on the loss of her husband, Johnson wrote: "Whom I have lost let me not now remember." Who could mistake the meaning? "You have lost your husband, but see all *I* have lost—losses I dare not think of." That is to say, his own wife, his mother, etc. Then he added that others had suffered also—"Lucy Porter has just lost her brother." But no; he was thinking of Thrale, whom he wished not even to "now remember," though he was at the moment remembering him, and dwelling on his merits.

Some of the editor's facetious comments are not very intelligible. Mrs Thrale wrote of her husband that "he had not much heart, and his fair daughters none at all." This, the editor good-naturedly says, "she recorded, or *pretended* to record, in her journal." The eldest of his five daughters, he adds, was sixteen, and the youngest only two years old. Every one knows that there are affectionate children, even at these ages, as well as heartless ones, or there are indications of these qualities. We have then this mysterious utterance concerning the youngest: "She died two years later—not five years old—*and without a heart*"! I cannot guess what this means.

Dr B. Hill is a rather indifferent hand at translation. Witness his dealing with the familiar "*omne ignotum pro magnifico*," which means that "everything unknown is taken to be splendid." But the editor has it, "the unknown always passes for something *peculiarly* grand." Macaulay's "form boy" would surely do better than this.

Johnson once visited a toyshop. We are actually furnished in a note with his definition of a toyshop, taken from the Dictionary, "a shop where playthings and little nice manufactures are sold."

THE EDITOR AND MRS PIOZZI.

DR B. HILL'S animosity to Mrs Piozzi, and indeed to most of the ladies who figure in his chronicle, is extraordinary. She was a forger, a fabricator of letters, and a clumsy fabricator too. For his charges there is hardly any foundation, save in his own morbid imaginings. There seems a lack of literary propriety in thus assailing a pleasant, volatile woman, whose little failings were more or less privileged, and were treated indulgently by one greater than the editor. What will be said of this? When her husband was ill she used to write his "franks" for him. In this, the editor actually assures us solemnly, she was guilty of felony, "*and had incurred the penalty of seven years' transportation* (vide *Gentleman's Magazine*, 1764)," for in 1783, a young gentleman was sentenced for this very offence. The reader need not be reminded that the cases were utterly different, the felony of the latter being the imitating a member's name with some criminal intent, either to defraud the revenue or the member in question. Mrs Piozzi did it, of course, with her husband's sanction, as an amanuensis. But it is childish discussing such a point.

On another occasion, in January 1783, she had written from Bath a distracted letter as to her children—"Harriet is dead, Cicely is dying," —on which the editor with much scorn: "Why she had left her dying child, and the other who was thought to be dying, to strangers to nurse she forgot to say." I can inform Dr B. Hill. One of her children was not dying, but had died some time before; for Johnson says, "I am glad you went to Streatham, though you could not save her,"—so she had not left her to strangers. The other child was at school at Kensington, and the reason the mother was not with her was that she herself was most seriously ill, as on getting into the chaise she was obliged to give up her journey to go back to her room.

In his ardour to prove the lady a "fabricator" of her own letters, the editor gets into strange confusion. Johnson had written a letter to Mrs Thrale, dated September 13, 1777, as to which the editor pronounces authoritatively, "This must be an answer to one of her's, dated five days later," that is, of September 18. So she had either misplaced the letter or altered or mistaken the date. He proves it in this way. In his letter of the 13th Johnson spoke of Queenie, and that she had no consumptive symptoms; Mrs Thrale was not to be alarmed, etc. He adds, "You must not let foolish fancies take hold on your imagination." In this, Dr B. Hill contends, Johnson refers to her letter of the 18th, where she had spoken of their alarm on finding they had "sat down thirteen to table."

He also mentioned a lady's son who was in danger, a *real* evil, not an imaginary one, as was Queenie's case Having in a preceding letter, dated the 8th, written of this lady and her son, he now comes back to the subject and moralises, adding, "Now I write again, having just received your letter dated the 10th." Thus here are three letters in regular order—the 8th, 10th, and 13th, all dealing with the same topic. It is clear, therefore, so far that the letter of the 13th is in its right place. Now for Mrs Thrale's answer of the 18th, which it is said should have come before Johnson's of the 13th. She writes that on the 17th they had sat down to table thirteen—a bad omen for Queenie—and Murphy had noted her hectic complexion. Hence the argument is that Johnson had answered that it was a "foolish fancy," that there was no danger of consumption, etc. But this is clearly an answer to Mrs Thrale's of the 10th (not given), in which, as we have seen, she had shown alarm.

But let us read the two letters, Johnson's and Mrs Thrale's, which follow each other, but are said to be misplaced. What will be said to this? At the end of Mrs Thrale's letter of the 18th, she writes, "Mr Thrale is cured of his passion for Lady R.," and Johnson answers her on the 20th, "Master is very inconstant to Lady R." In the same letter he writes, "Pretty dear Queenie, I hope you will never lose her, though I should *go to Lichfield* and she should sit thirteenth in many a company." Mrs Thrale had written on the 18th that something always happened when he went to Lichfield, and Johnson replies that she would still live though he *did* go to Lichfield, and she did sit thirteenth at many a table. Then Mrs Thrale writes, "How could I write so much, and from Streatham?" and Johnson answers, "You have nothing to say because you live at Streatham, and expect me to say much, etc." Thus here are *four* topics mentioned by Mrs Thrale, with four replies by Johnson. Surely *his* letter of the 20th is an answer to hers, and should not be placed *before* hers, as Dr B. Hill contends. The editor's speculation is therefore all wrong.

Dr B. Hill sometimes does not seem to understand or recognise the sage's turn of thought. Johnson wrote to Mrs Thrale that he had been much entertained by Bozzy's "Journal": "One would think the man had been hired to be a spy upon me." Surely this is "a pointed" utterance, forcible, Johnsonian, and quite in character, Wonderful to say, Dr B. Hill will not have it. But how did it get into one of Johnson's letters? Why, the woman forged it! Such is the critical faculty of our editor.

In one of Johnson's printed letters are found the words "futile pictures," which refer to Miss Knowles's embroideries. It was contended that what he really wrote was "sutile pictures." "This initial *s*, being always formed like an *f*, was here *absurdly* taken for one." Thus the editor. The point is a little perplexing, and it will be seen, quite escapes Dr B. Hill, who rather clouds the matter by the misstatement that Johnson always used this particular *s* at the beginning of a word. "Sutile" is certainly what one might expect Johnson to say; but here is the difficulty. The long *s*, which resembles an *f*, is used by Johnson only in the *middle* of a word, and indeed is almost always used by other writers with the double *s*. In the *fac-simile* letter supplied by Dr B. Hill we have the small *s* used four or five times by Johnson at the beginning of a word, as in "safely," "succeed," "separate," "so," and the long *s* used in the middle, as in "yourself." This seems almost conclusive, and at least disposes of the editor's statement that Johnson's "initial *s* was *always* formed like an *f*." There was no absurdity therefore in the case. One writer says that he had seen the original, and this "dark line had been put across the letter perhaps by the printer or corrector." But this again is doubtful enough. Printers or correctors do not thus alter original MS. Again, if "sutile" is Johnsonian, so is "futile." For to him these pictures thus worked or embroidered would seem a "futile" occupation enough.

Johnson appealed to friends to support "a benefit for a gentlewoman of——"—the name of the place being illegible. The editor thinks that the word "is something like Lournitz," which, he speculates, "is perhaps the name of the place in South Wales whence Miss Williams came." Thus it *may be* Lournitz; and Lournitz *may be* the place from which Miss Williams came. But apart from these two wonderful "may be's," a "gentlewoman of Lournitz" would be no claim for relief. The word was clearly descriptive. "A gentlewoman of position" or of good birth, for the next words are "distressed by blindness."

JOHNSONIAN MISCELLANIES.

Dr B. Hill, having disposed of Boswell's "Life" and Johnson's "Letters," was engaged on what was to be "the work of my life," an edition of Johnson's masterpiece, the "Lives of the Poets," when Mr Leslie Stephen interposed, and somewhat adroitly suggested that he should turn aside and take up the noting of something less pretentious. Was there not Murphy, Hoole, Tom Tyers, Piozzi & Co., and such small fry? Why not note *them?* The editor eagerly accepted the suggestion. Hence these miscellanies. It seems these were ready three years ago. An impatient public was clamouring all the time for the work; and though we are told of "the necessity of passing all my winters abroad, on the banks of the Lake of Geneva, or on the shores of the Mediterranean," he felt it a duty to satisfy these desires. For an editor, "*however he may be supported by the climate*," has in such a situation to struggle with difficulties. This support of the climate is, after all, but a negative one when you are writing or noting a book, and no amount of climatic aid will supply other deficiencies. There was no need, however, for such pressing haste, for this collection has virtually been before the public for some forty years, and in another shape for some ten years, Mr Croker having supplied us with his well-known and now scarce "Johnsoniana," which Mr Napier reprinted.

Dr B. Hill, as usual, enlarges, with great minuteness, and in rather pathetic fashion, on "the difficulties" above alluded to, notably about the history of a certain "box of books," Dr B. Hill's own working tools, without which he is stranded. The box contained, we may imagine, Walpole—himself a boxful—the *Rambler*, and the other *necessary* things. It was "despatched from London to Alassio on the Riviera," where they were anxiously awaited. "It was not till full five weeks after my arrival that they reached me. Fifty-nine days had they spent" on the road. This was very bad, and it tells the tale of railway neglect sufficiently. But in the bitterness of his soul our editor makes some further dismal calculations. "They had advanced at the rate of about three-quarters of a mile an hour. They were taken to Clarens, on the

Lake of Geneva," and so on. True, there were other boxes of books which "used to creep at a somewhat faster pace"; and the whole culminates in the assurance that "the Kentish carrier, who, leaving Rochester betimes, delivered that same day a gammon of bacon and two razes of ginger as far as Charing Cross, was making more expedition." With all this, of course, Johnsonian readers have no concern. 'Tis a matter of "reclamation" to the railway authorities, but, as we know by this time, it is the editor's way. It is his way also not to see that the case of the Shakespeare carriers does not illustrate his case, for to carry goods from Rochester to Charing Cross some forty miles, and in the one day, was "good going." Gibbon, we are assured, when he brought over his great library to Lausanne, hardly suffered more than our editor did with his box of books.

The editor has an uneasy feeling that there are cavilling fault-finders, who, in their scurvy way, are ready to detect flaws: so he promptly "takes the bull by the horns" in a new and highly ingenious fashion. Mistakes, of course, there are; but it is all owing to the pernicious system of printing books that now obtains. "The imperfections of a work such as this is, are often *more clearly seen by the editor* than by the most *sharp*-sighted critic." An ingenious turn, as who should say, "I knew it all the time, and much better than *you*." "Mistakes are discovered too late for correction, but not for criticism." There, we see, is the grievance, which can only be remedied in this way: "Were the whole book in type, and *cost of no moment*, what improvements could be made." In fact, our editor would like to begin the whole work of rewriting when the proofs were in his hands. Give him but a free hand then, and all will be well. As he tells us, "I have never yet finished an index without wishing that, by the help of it, I could edit and re-edit my work."

But by a hard fate, these things are not permissible. Cost *is* of moment; and the directors of the Clarendon Press would decidedly object to what the editor so gently terms, "improvements being made." The odd part of all this is, that three-fourths of the volumes are all secure from correction, having been written by other people, and possibly three-fourths of the notes are quotations; so what the "pother" is about it is hard to say. True, old-fashioned, behind-date writers contrive to do with a system of *writing* the book before it goes to the printer; they alter, write, and rewrite, have it copied and typed, with the result that they do not want to alter anything when the print is before them.

Notwithstanding "the support of the climate," the editor has committed many mistakes, which I shall now proceed to point out, for the book teems with the old faults of misapprehension, delusion, and hurried and imperfect reference, and for which the difficulties of the situation are hardly accountable. To begin, there is a quotation from Gibbon, the point of which is mistaken: "Tillemont's accuracy," says the editor in his preface, "may, as Gibbon says, be *inimitable;* but none the less, inspired by the praise which our great historian bestows on mere accuracy, a scholar should never lose the hope of imitation." It may be presumed that the editor refers to the note in chapter xlvii., when Gibbon writes, "And here I must take leave for ever of the incomparable guide, whose bigotry is over-balanced by the merits of erudition, diligence, veracity, and scrupulous minuteness." Now here "our great historian" wrote that Tillemont was "incomparable," not "inimitable," a different thing, and he gave him praise, not for his *mere* "accuracy," but for other admirable gifts. The editor's point was that he might "imitate"; that word changed, his point is gone.

The editor tells us how "Joseph Andrews" had been translated into Russian, which leads on to this truly mysterious announcement. "Strangely enough"—we should here naturally expect something about English books in Russia —"strangely enough, a railway station is called in Russian *Vauxhall*, after the famous Gardens in ———,"—where shall we suppose?—"*in Chelsea*"*!* Joseph Andrews, railway station, and the Vauxhall Gardens in Chelsea!

But here is an astonishing misapprehension. Johnson said, when on his deathbed, "I should have roared for my book as Othello did for his handkerchief." Every one at all familiar with the play will know this passage, viz. that in scene iv., act iii., where Othello answers Desdemona again and again with, "The handkerchief! The handkerchief!" This was the "roaring for"—that is, demanding incessantly the article. But no, the editor thinks only of the word "roar," not of the thing, and seriously assures us that "Johnson refers to act v., scene ii., where Emilia says to Othello, 'Now lay thee down and *roar*,'" that is, invites him to roar, which he does not do. In this state of things some sort of misgiving occurs to the editor that he is not going right, so he insinuates that it was Johnson who was wrong; for "it was not for the handkerchief that Othello roared, as he did not as yet know the trick that had been played him"! But Johnson was referring to the passage where he did roar.

Among Johnson's visitors when he was dying was a Mrs Davies, whose name is mentioned several times by Hoole, and spelt in that way. No one could doubt that the wife of Tom Davies, the bookseller, was meant. But the editor opines: "Most probably she was the Mrs Dav*is* that was 'about Mrs Williams.'" But Mrs Williams had now been dead nearly two years, so this person was not likely to be there. Further, Mrs Davies dined with Johnson and his friends, and seemed to be treated as a lady. Tom Davies also, her husband, was writing to the dying sage at the time, sent him pork, etc., and naturally sent his wife to see him. I am not surprised that the editor at last falteringly adds: "Perhaps, however, she was the wife of Tom Davies."

With the plain meaning of a passage "leaping to his very eyes," the editor will rather perversely seize on some erratic meaning. "I wrote," said Johnson to G. Steevens, "the first line" (of a poem) "in that small house beyond the church [at Hampstead]." "By enclosing Hampstead in brackets," explains the editor, "he apparently wishes to show that it was *there* that Johnson told him the fact." This is surely not the meaning; it was to show *where* the "small house" and church were, and not the place where Johnson was speaking in. He might have used the phrase "in that small house," in London itself.

Here is an *excursus* on Johnson's putting a lump of sugar in his glass of port wine. Did he do this or did he not? "It is not to be supposed that when he drank his three bottles of port at University College, he put a lump of sugar *into every one of his thirty-six glasses.*" Granted; but the reason is the odd one, not that there are not anything like thirty-six glasses in three bottles, or that he only took this sugar "sometimes," but "no Oxford common-room *would have stood it.*" Further, and what is a more serious thing, "Boswell makes no mention of *this sugar.*"

Johnson, as we know, was displeased with Garrick for not helping him in his "Shakespeare," by lending him early editions, and made no mention of him in the preface. "He *did worse*," says the editor—always ready to have a fling at the sage—"than not mention him. He reflected on him, though not by name, 'as a not very communicative collector of rare copies.'" This is rather a perversion of the text; for Johnson had spoken generally. "I have not found *the collectors* of such rarities very communicative." There is a class of persons named, and there is not the invidiousness that Dr B. Hill would make out. Further, the point whether the books were refused to Johnson was disputed by the owner.

Hannah More reported a good story of Johnson's and Boswell's enthusiasm on passing by Macbeth's "blasted heath," and finding next morning that it was a mistake, and not the actual scene. He himself told this to her. "There seems to be some mistake in her narrative," says the editor, who then quotes passages from the "Journey" and "Tour," to *prove* how the travellers had actually driven over the very heath, and got to Forres, etc. Surely this does not affect the story. They had mistaken the locality first, and later came to the true place. On such occasions Dr B. Hill seems to get befogged.

Here is a mysterious gloss. Johnson writes that, "I then went to Streatham and had many stops," *i.e.* either interruptions or haltings by the way. The editor, however, sees deeper. "I conjecture that he means *obstructions* or *impediments in the mind*, part of what he calls 'my old disease of mind.'" Curious "stops" these!

In a letter of Johnson's, the editor tells us, "I suspected the words, 'most sincerely yours,' for I had never known it thus used by Johnson." A very fair criticism. Scrutinising the original MS., he found that the words were "not clear, but I believe that it is 'zealously yours.'" Who will conceive of the sage signing himself "*zealously* yours"? And surely the editor ought to "suspect" these words also—for his own reason, that he had never known them used by Johnson, or by any one else in the world.

The editor, making one of his "discoveries," calls attention to three letters of Johnson's, which he got from Mr Pearson, the autograph dealer, and elaborately proves that they were written to Richardson, the novelist. But a single glance will show it. "I wish," No. 2 runs, "Sir Charles (Grandison) had not compromised it in the matter of religion." It also asks for an account of "the translations of 'Clarissa' which *you have*," and speaks of new volumes coming out, "Grandison" being published in instalments.

A Hibernian gentleman was once extolling his countryman Burke, and expatiated on his going down into the bowels of the earth in a bag, and how he took care of his clothes, for he "went down in a bag." In short, it was "*Burke in a bag*," as Johnson ludicrously put it. All which is absurd enough; but the editor must caution us. "The bag, *apparently*, was not *the vehicle* in which he went down, but a covering for his clothes." Only "apparently"? There is no doubt of it. The editor is fearful lest there be persons who imagine that the great orator was let down in "*a vehicle*" formed of a bag, much as coals or flour would be sent down. So anxious is he to prevent mistake, that he looks out in his Dictionary the word "sack," which has not been introduced at all, and tells us that "*sack* was used for a woman's loose robe." Still bag is not sack, and a woman's loose robe is not a bag; and this was a *bag* pure and simple.

The editor is puzzled by a phrase of Johnson's, "by a catch." "I do not know," he says, "in what sense he uses this word. Perhaps he means by a sudden impulse, by something that caught hold of him." It is curious that so thorough a Johnsonian should not recall another occasion when the same word was used: "God Almighty will not take a catch of him"—that is, will not take him by surprise; take an unfair advantage of him.

A poor woman is described in the text as "sitting shivering in a niche" of the old Westminster Bridge. This is surely intelligible—these niches with seats are still to be seen on Vauxhall and other bridges. But this is not enough. To prevent all mistake, the editor begins with a definition of "niche," taken from the Dictionary. "Johnson defines 'niche' as a hollow in which a statue may be placed"! Though in the case of the bridge there were *seats*, for the woman was sitting there. The editor, who seems to think that the poor woman had no business to be there at all, in a place which Dr Johnson had proved was intended for a statue, now introduces from Dodsley's "Account of London" a passage about these very recesses, which, he says, states that they were "intended to be filled with groups of statuary." The woman must now really move on. But having Dodsley's work on my own shelves—an entertaining book—I took it down, and read, to my astonishment, not that these recesses were intended for statues, but that "*between* the recesses are *pedestals*," on which groups of statuary were to be placed. So the whole niche speculation utterly fails.

Another odd mistake. In 1765 Johnson wrote down, "I read my resolutions." The editor fancies that he was thinking of some old resolutions made thirteen years before, "perhaps the resolutions made when his wife lay dead before him." Nothing of the kind. Turning back to only the *preceding* page, we find them: "*My resolutions*, which God perfect," *i.e.* "to avoid loose thoughts and rise at light."

At Pembroke College Johnson, showing his old haunts and going over the place, pointed out the old scenes: "Here we played cricket," etc. This is not by the card. "Johnson must have pointed to a field *outside* the college precincts, *for within there was no room for cricket.*" A needless caution. It would have occurred to no one that cricket was played "within the precincts," *i.e.* in a courtyard.

Every one knows the story of how Johnson knocked down his bookseller, Osborne, with a folio. The scene took place in Johnson's own room. It is not of much importance what the volume was, but Nichols identified it as a copy of the Septuagint. But the editor has a fancy which must be introduced. It seems that Osborne had made Johnson a present of a "Second Folio Shakespeare": and the editor has the fantastic notion that either by design or chance, Johnson had used this tome to *terraser* his visitor! True, he hesitates somewhat, for "it is scarcely likely that Osborne would have brought it to Johnson, as schoolboys used to provide birch rods, with which they were beaten." But this "conceit," such as it is, seemed so taking and pleasant, that we find him in another work stating more positively, "in the good old days in the grammar schools the unhappy culprit was often required to provide a birch rod, etc. Might not Osborne in like manner have provided a folio with which he was to be knocked down?" Now we have heard in schools of boys having to *ask* for punishment, and it may be to *fetch* the birch rod, but it may be doubted if there was ever a custom of the boys being sent out to *purchase* a birch rod! But this by the way. Then as to Nichols, who was so positive? All a mistake, for the editor has seen the sale catalogue of Johnson's books, and there was no Septuagint among them; so he still clings to his "Second Folio Shakespeare." This interesting relic has come into the fitting hands of Sir Henry Irving, who is an accomplished *virtuoso*, and he has written to the editor on the subject; so "*may it not be that Sir Henry Irving's treasure is the great historic folio?*" It certainly may not by any manner of means be. For, after all his doubts and speculations, the editor knows perfectly where the book is to be found. "A Greek Bible, I *must admit*, was left by him to a friend," surely a sufficient reason for his not finding it in the sale catalogue. It is described in the will as "Michelius' Greek Testament" (the name should be *W*ichelius), and this was bequeathed to his friend Strahan. Nichols also names a Greek Testament, so the proof is strong and complete. Dr B. Hill murmurs something about its being unlikely that so correct a man "would have made so profane a use" of the sacred volume—another "conceit."

We sometimes "startle" ("Bozzy's" good word) at a phrase of our editor, as when speaking of Dr Hawesworth, who had committed suicide on the ill success of his book, he says: "A man who had received £6000 for a mere compilation *was scarcely justified* in putting an end to his life." Scarcely justified! Not orthodox this. But we are relieved on finding that it was a sort of mild joke. "He should have left suicide to his publishers, who were great losers." This jesting is out of place.

Here is a sort of discovery—or "no discovery" rather, for the editor's elucidation of a knotty point is, as usual, all wrong. A young lady of much personal charm, it was stated, had perpetrated a solecism, "for all her father is now become a nobleman, and excessively rich." Who was the young lady, and who the nobleman? "Perhaps Lord Sandys," the editor tells us, "who became a nobleman the year after his marriage." Now at once we can see that he is astray in this speculation. For the young lady was described as grown up when her father became a nobleman; whereas, if it be Lord Sandys, she could only have been just born when he became a nobleman. We need not, therefore, go any further, leaving Dr B. Hill thus to dispose of his own theory.

Who was the dying Jenny? Johnson in one of his note-books mentions this person, for whom he paid 5s. 3d. to a clergyman to attend on her last sickness. "Was she some poor outcast like the one he had carried home," etc. She was probably some retainer or maid-servant, which is all that any one would wish to know—if so much. But the editor, in his preface, bewails his fate in not being able to "throw light," as he puts it, on the great matter. "Who was dying Jenny?" It does not matter. Even did we know, we should not gain much.

The editor generally contrives, where he has a choice, to select the wrong thing. Johnson had said that "Greek was like lace; every one gets as much of it as he can." A capital illustration and intelligible too. Most ladies are proud of their bit of old lace, "point," or Brussels; it is cherished, and seems to give a sort of distinction. People of even moderate taste will be glad "to get as much of it as they can," and it will fetch a fancy price. But our editor assures us gravely that the lace Johnson was speaking of was the common cheap gold lace or braid found on gentlemen's coat-cuffs and collars! Amazing! A thing that is of no value at all! Imagine people "getting as much" of this stuff as they can! Then he must furnish quotations from "Irene," Ruddiman, Lord Chesterfield, Joseph Andrews, and Jeremy Bentham to prove —what? That gold lace was *worn* in those days!

"Nor were our conversations," says Hawkins, "like that of the Rota Club, restrained to," etc. On which the editor: "Hawkins, *I suppose*, refers to the *Rota* Club, in which," etc. Of course he does, for he says he does.

The editor is always rather weak when he would be sarcastic. Mr Cradock mentions a dinner at which were the Duke of Cumberland and Johnson, which Mr Croker is inclined to doubt. "It is hardly possible that Dr Johnson should have met the Duke of Cumberland without Boswell having mentioned it." This was reasonable criticism enough. But hearken further. Dr B. Hill: "Mr Croker forgets that there are men who can dine with a Duke, and *not boast of it*." Who denidges of it? No one could suppose that Johnson would *boast* of meeting great folk, and Mr Croker did not suppose it. But how natural that Johnson would tell "Bozzy" what he thought of so remarkable a personage as the Duke of Cumberland. His account would have been a most interesting one, and to none more so than to Dr B. Hill.

There is one word that the editor has vainly looked for in the great Dictionary, viz. "Spavined." Most readers know what a spavined animal is, and most readers would be content to know that it meant a disease in a horse's leg. True, the editor admits plaintively, "*He only* gives 'spavin.'" That surely will do us very well, and help us on to "spavined."

The editor is inclined to depreciate Reynolds, who, as the world knows, was the most amiable, engaging, and popular of men. He was an admirable family man, affectionate, kind, charitable. But to our astonishment, the editor announces that "he seems to have had but little sympathy with his sisters." By way of establishing this, he quotes an abusive letter from one, a Mrs Johnson, who cast him off because he would not be "converted," and repent of his sins. It is also stated that this lady refused his offer to take her son and teach him his own art—an odd way of his showing "little sympathy." "Renny," the other sister, lived with him for many years, until her "tiresome fidgetiness," Miss Burney tells us, and general nagging, made them part company. She then proposed that he should give up his house at Richmond to her, to be her property, though she would allow him to use it—a proposal he rejected, from his "little sympathy." Again, Reynolds had invited Boswell to dine with him at Painters' Stainers' Hall, "as you love," he said, "to see life in all its modes. I will (call for you) about two; the blackguards dine at half an hour after." From which the editor extracts the theory that Reynolds, who dined always at five, was exasperated at having to go and dine at two! that he used "strong language" in consequence, "perhaps owing to his vexation at losing two or three hours of his working day." And further, "none of his hours were spent in idleness, or lost in dissipation." All which is a dream, and disposed of by the fact that Reynolds could have declined the invitation if he chose; that he was so willing to go that he brought a friend with him; that he used no "strong" language, for by "blackguards" he humorously alluded to the fraternity to which he himself belonged, or to the inferior branch of the profession. As to none of his hours "being spent in idleness, or lost in dissipation," if this refers to a dinner, it is notorious that he dined out, and spent much time at the club, at Garrick's, and was, in fact, *recherché* everywhere.

Johnson's happy jest on the *congé d'élire* leads the editor to a general examination of this thorny subject. He must first, of course, hurry to his "Johnson's Dictionary," and after a due definition of the words, takes us next to—but no one will guess whither—to the Dr Hampden of modern times—the well-known Bishop of Hereford! We have *his* case and *his congé d'élire*, Lord John Russell's letter, and details of the case generally. Not content with this, he follows the heretical bishop to Bow Church, describes the scene there, the "citation," the "objectors," etc. All very interesting, no doubt, and one of those "fascinating anecdotes" that so delight Mr Leslie Stephen, but still out of place here.

In the editor's ardour to point out blunders—and he does so with great severity—he often stumbles into mistakes himself. Thus, when Mr Cradock describes his meeting Johnson at an undated dinner at the Literary Club, and says that he thought it suggested the "Retaliation" to Goldsmith, Dr B. Hill exclaims: "Such a blunder as this shows that not much trust can be placed in his account," his point being, that Cradock's *first time* of meeting Johnson was in 1776, while Goldsmith had died in 1774. On turning to this gentleman's account, we find that all he says is that it was the first time he "*dined in company*" with Johnson, not the first time he had met him; and this first meeting might have been before Goldsmith's death. It is the same with his remarks on the Cheshire Cheese, where some old gentlemen *habitués* were mentioned by Mr Jay as having remembered Johnson. Mr Jay, who wrote in the 'fifties, spoke of this, describing Johnson, when in Gough Square and Bolt Court, as frequenting the Cheese, and when at the Temple, the Mitre, because he did not like to cross the street. Dr B. Hill is scornful on this "loose talk." How could they remember Johnson in Gough Square, when he left it nearly a hundred years before? The editor has misapprehended the context. Some antediluvians remembered Johnson himself, but the rest of the story was merely the tradition picked up in the Tavern. The "old gentlemen" did not say that they remembered the Doctor at Gough Square.

Prepared as we are for Dr B. Hill's strange *capriccios*, we scarcely expected that he would gravely set himself to making a regular *exegesis* of a dinner *menu*. He actually proceeds to edit for us a bill of fare! Johnson had set down in Latin the items of his last dinner at Streatham, in translating which Dr B. Hill falls into what seem surprising mistakes. There was, it seems, for dinner a roast leg of lamb and spinach, "*crus coctum cum herbis*," etc. We have also a turkey, and a "*farcimen farinaceum cum uvis passis*," which the editor interprets as "the stuffing" of the lamb, I suppose, made of flour and raisins. A strange dish certainly, which must have made the Doctor uncomfortable. No wonder that our commentator says almost pathetically, "I have looked in vain in an old cookery book for a receipt for '*farcimen farinaceum cum uvis*,'" though had he looked at all he might have consulted other cookery books. He adds: "Perhaps Mrs Thrale *had ordered her favourite sauce*." Whether she did so or not the whole that remains is dark. A fresh wonder: "*It seems odd* that the lamb and turkey were not *followed by a pudding or sweets*"! Odd or not, the editor is rather abroad here. The "*farcimen farinaceum*" was surely not stuffing for the lamb or turkey (I feel the absurdity of discussing such trivialities), but, it is distinctly stated, was another dish altogether—possibly that very pudding, the absence of which the editor so much laments. A glance at the Latin will show this. We construe it: "A flour dumpling with raisins." He assuredly mistranslates. Then Miss Austen is introduced with a dissertation on "Courses," with quotations from her novels, and so on in the usual way.

I shall live *mihi carior*, wrote Johnson. "Perhaps," the editor says, "he had on his mind Juvenal's line, '*Carior est illis homo quam sibi*.'" Certainly not; for here the meaning is the direct opposite: the man is dearer to *others* than to himself. This would be sufficient. But no. What Johnson "had in his mind"—indeed what every fourth or fifth form boy would have in his mind—is the passage in Ovid: "O me! mihi carior."

It is truly strange that the editor would not know so familiar a thing.

The sort of cloud or fog in which the editor fashions his notes is shown by the following:—As is well known, Johnson put a definition in his Dictionary of "Renegado"—"one who deserts"—"a revolter"—"sometimes we say a '*Gower*,'" meaning to point at the peer of that name, who had deserted the Jacobites. "*This is made clearer*," says the editor, "by the following passage from the 'Lives of the Norths':—'Many of the Turks think that the Gowers (Giaours), or unbelievers, are unworthy,'" etc. This is ludicrous. Johnson was not thinking of the Eastern word, "Giaour," nor was North thinking of "Gower," the peer. Nothing is "made clearer," save that the two passages have no connection.

Mrs Montagu showed Johnson some plates that had once belonged to Queen Elizabeth. He paid her a compliment, saying they had no reason to be ashamed of their present possessor. The editor seems to trace some more occult influence in the names, for his remark is, "Mrs Montagu's name was Elizabeth."

Mention is made of two boxing men, Mendoza and "Big Ben." This was not long after Johnson's death. The editor conceives that it was probably after him that Dr Benjamin Symonds, who was warden of Wadham in Dr B. Hill's undergraduate days, was called "Big Ben." That is to say, about the 'forties some one was going about bearing a nickname acquired about 1790. Surely the editor ought to know that "Big Ben" is a common *soubriquet*. "Big Ben" of Westminster was so called after Sir Benjamin Hall. Any extra stout person, of the name of Benjamin, is likely enough to be called "Big Ben," without going back to a boxer of the eighteenth century.

Murphy, in his perfunctory narrative, says that Johnson never talked of Garrick "without a tear in his eyes"—either a misprint for "eyes" or for "tears." The editor thinks it a matter important enough to stop and have his little joke—"allowing that one tear can be in both eyes."

There are three words for which the editor has a sort of penchant, and is passionately eager to prove that in the last century they were used in the sense they are now. First, we had "respectable" as a term of praise, and a long list of instances was furnished in "The Life." He comes back to it in another of his books, still eager to show that it was a term of praise, that is, a person deserving of respect, and quotes yet more authorities. "Eminent," too, we all know. Eminent statesmen, eminent writers, or preachers, etc. But the editor thinks we are in the dark, and gives us a sheaf of quotations. "The following instances show its use," and it is *proved* to us beyond cavil, that people then spoke of "an eminent personage," "eminent merchant," "eminent man," etc.

Of the use of "polluted" in the sense of "stained," "soiled," etc., the editor also gives a collection of illustrations. So fascinated is he with the word, that he returns to it again. "To the instances given of the use of 'polluted' I would add," etc., and he quotes, "Dryden polluted his page," "Pope polluted his wit," and so on.

Mrs Thrale mentions an appeal to Johnson, as to pronunciation, whether it should be "irrepărable" or "irrep*air*able." Johnson decided that it was long. Is it not clear that Mrs Thrale was merely spelling the word phonetically? But the editor insists that Mrs Thrale seems to have thought that the syllable "pa," in "paro," was long. The poor lady gave no opinion at all, she merely reported Johnson's.

The editor has an odd notion of what "borrowing" is. Johnson's phrase, "the wits of Charles" (*i.e.* of Charles II.'s time) he traced to Addison. It was "borrowed" from the *Spectator*, where we find "the wits of King Charles's time." Surely this is mere statement, and could not be set down in another way. We might as well say "Mr Gladstone at Hawarden" was borrowed from "Mr Gladstone at Hawarden Castle."

Johnson said that, when he was writing his Dictionary, no less than 160 quires of the MS. had been written by mistake on both sides of the paper. It cost him £20, he said, to have it copied afresh on one side. "This must be a mistake," the editor says, "as were it only a shilling a quire, it would not nearly come to the sum," *i.e.* £8. It is the editor, however, who has fallen into the mistake, having counted only 160 quires. It should be double that number, as double the amount of paper was used, *i.e.* 320 quires, which would make £16, and allowing something for wider writing, this would nearly come up to Johnson's figure.

"The little girl poked her head." Imagine a grave commentator, "a scholar" too, stopping here to discuss this important "poking" of the little girl's head! The *only* definition given by Johnson of *poke*, is "to feel in the dark—to search." What are we to do? How get on with *only* this one definition? We must only leave the little girl to poke her head as best she can.

Lady Di Middleton, who espied Johnson in church on their Scotch tour, and who had known him in town, the editor tells us, "was perhaps of the family of the Earl of Middleton, who, in 1693, *threw in his lot* with James II." No. She was sister to Lord Stamford, and married an Edinburgh barrister, Mr Middleton, who later succeeded to the Middleton estates.

The editor sometimes disposes of his own argument or illustration, by setting down something that he never intended. Thus he relates how Mrs Gastrell got Johnson to read aloud the passage, "We have *heard* with our ears," to find out whether he would pronounce it "hēērd" or "herd." He shows that Johnson voiced it "hēērd," who said that to pronounce it "herd" "was nonsense." He likewise told Boswell that it should be "hēērd," because "herd" would be the single exception to the general sounding of the syllable "ear." He also told Mrs Gastrell that there was but one word of that sound in the language, viz. "herd" (of cattle). Which is all plain enough. But the editor gets into sad confusion over it. He tells us that the speech to Mrs Gastrell (as to there being but one word "herd," etc.) "seems a contradiction of what he told Boswell." How? He was talking to him about "hēēred" not "herd." Then, though he shows plainly that Johnson rejected "herd," he makes him say that to call it "hēērd" was nonsense! The editor meant to write "hēērd."

Johnson's well-known description of an actor's conversation, as "a renovation of hope," etc., was assumed by Mr Croker to refer to Sheridan; by John Taylor to Macklin; Macklin was also named, I think, by Malone. The editor discards these authorities, and prefers a newspaper! "According to the Edinburgh *Courant* of June 16, 1792, this was Macklin."

The editor has an ingenious fashion of minimising his mistakes. In a previous edition we have Johnson saying, when some one asked his opinion of a play called "Dido," "I never did the man an injury, yet he would read his tragedy to me." The editor speculated that this was one Lucas, who "had just been with me; he has compelled me to read his tragedy." These, it is clear, were different persons, for in the one case Johnson had to *listen* to the play; in the other he read it himself. In his note the editor says that Lucas was the author of "Dido," and that both instances referred to the same person. Now, however, he finds—no doubt from the "Biographia Dramatica," which he might have consulted at first—that Reed was the author of "Dido." "In a note I suggested that he" (Lucas) "may have been the author mentioned above; but in this I was mistaken, for it was Isaac Reed." It is something to have the editor crying *peccavi* in this way; but why such capriciousness in the selection? Why ignore the hundreds of mistakes that have been pointed out in his editions?

We are told that Burke was so vehement in arguing some patriotic questions, that "he would turn away so as to throw the end of his own tail into the face of his neighbour." The editor seems to caution us not to take this for a real "caudal appendage," for he tell us: "Burke, *no doubt, wore his hair tied up in a pigtail.*" Not a doubt of it. What else could he mean?

There are some strange mistakes about Beckford. Of a Jamaica gentleman then lately dead, Johnson said, "He will, whither he is now gone, not find much difference as to climate or to company." And again, on learning the death of a celebrated West Indian planter, "He is gone where he will not find the country warmer and the men much blacker than *that he has left.*" In both places the editor explains: "Perhaps (or probably) Alderman Beckford." Not at all. The man of whom Johnson was speaking had died out at Jamaica, "the country he had left." Beckford died in England, to which he had come in his boyhood. He was not "a celebrated West India planter," but a celebrated London politician, who had been Lord Mayor.

"A valuable edition of Bailey's Dictionary" is mentioned, which prompts the editor to make this observation: "It is not easy to see how *any* edition of Bailey could be valuable." First, is not that a dictionary of some value which Johnson used as the basis of his own? Second, it was issued as a small volume; then in two huge ones. The allusion was not to the merits of the book, but to its shape, *format*, binding, it might be.

The editor often takes a narrow view of people's motives and acts. Johnson sent a guinea to one Faden, son of a printer, whom he had known thirty years before, and who had lent him a guinea. "Faden," the editor tells us, "for a few weeks had a share in the *Universal Chronicle*, in which *The Idler* was published, *so that he could have stopped the guinea out of the money due to Johnson*"*!* As is said in one of Ibsen's pieces, "People don't do such things."

The editor misapprehends the plainest passage. Boswell, when about to publish the "Life," hesitated as to the terms. Would he sell the book "out and out," or "I should incline to *game*, as Sir Joshua says"—*i.e.* speculate on the profits. But the editor has this odd theory. Boswell was thinking of Sir Joshua's use of the word "game"! "Perhaps *gamble* . . . was in constant use, and Reynolds *was singular in sticking to an old-fashioned word.*" As to "gamble" being in constant use, the editor disposes of *that* by assuring us that it is *not* found in the Dictionary. So that "game" was the only word he could have used. It is impossible to deal seriously with these delusions.

Johnson was sometimes reminded by his friends that he was too dictatorial in his talk, a reproof which he took kindly, and would, in answer to what "they called the pride of learning, *say* that it was of a defensive kind." The editor must assure us that "they borrowed this ('the defensive pride') from Johnson," and quotes another passage, "mine was of the defensive kind." Now their speech had nothing to do with "defensive pride"; *that* was Johnson's answer, so they "borrowed" nothing from him. It is clear the editor thought that "say" referred to them.

"I never but once," said Johnson, "*balked* an invitation to dinner." Surely intelligible; he never "balked" the hospitable intention of the inviter. The editor goes to the *third* meaning of the word in the Dictionary, "to omit, or refuse anything." But he passes by the first and strict meaning, "to frustrate or disappoint," which is the fitting one here.

Dr Percy seems to be one of the circle to whom the editor has a strong dislike. The Bishop tells how Johnson had some disputes in early life with Lord Lyttelton, "which so improperly influenced him in his life of that worthy nobleman"—a temperate criticism. But, as usual, the editor dips deep to find lower motives for Percy's "prejudice." Was he not chaplain to the King? Was he not devoted to the Duke of Northumberland? His wife had been nurse to one of the princes, etc. So he was "naturally shocked at Johnson's ridicule of a worthy nobleman." It is well known that Johnson's treatment of Lyttelton was not considered handsome by his contemporaries. Percy, moreover, was not "shocked" at all—he deprecated Johnson's "prejudice"—nor was he shocked at Johnson's "ridicule," for in Johnson's article there is no ridicule of Lyttelton.

Again, Percy tells us that when Johnson was casting about for a title, he suddenly thought of "The Rambler." "It would be difficult," says Percy, "to find any other that so exactly coincided with the motto he had adopted on the title-page." Most strangely, the editor says: "Percy *seems to think* that Johnson *chose his motto first, and then cast about for a title to suit it.*" Percy uses the phrases, "He *has* adopted," and "It would be difficult to find." It is clear that it was he himself that was passing judgment on the transaction as a whole, and not Johnson. Johnson chose a motto, and Percy notes that the title suited the motto.

Hannah More writes that "Mr Boswell was here last night; he perfectly adores Johnson." On which the editor: "Boswell, who keeps his narrative so closely to what concerns Johnson, does not mention this." Exactly. In any case, how was Boswell to "mention" "I adored Johnson," etc.? The editor fancied that Johnson was there with Boswell, but is mistaken; he was not. On his own showing, Boswell was therefore justified in saying nothing of the occasion.

Johnson very complacently dwelt on the poets, other literary lights, who had belonged to his college. "Sir, we are a nest of singing birds." Among these was Shenstone. Dr B. Hill gives *his* meed of praise also: "Among *my* contemporaries were Dr Edwin Hutch, Dr Moore, and Canon Dixon, author of finer poems than were sung by *most* of the last century singing birds." "Sung by most." These Dixon poems are hardly so well known as they should be. And Hutch and Moore?

"It was in 1739 that Swift was asked to get Johnson the degree of M.A. of Dublin." There is no certainty that Swift was asked. Pope asked Lord Gower, who asked a friend to ask Swift.

Hawkins mentions a gentleman who, laying out his grounds picturesquely, was obliged to apply to a neighbour (for leave to plant, etc.) with whom he was not upon cordial terms. The editor imagines that this was the case of

Shenstone and Lord Lyttelton, who were not on cordial terms. This seems far-fetched.

"In the words of a great scholar of the North, who did not like him, he (Johnson) spoke in the Lincolnshire dialect." "The great scholar," says the editor, "was perhaps Lord Monboddo." This judge, however, was no "great scholar," but a philosopher. Nor could he know anything about "the Lincolnshire dialect." "The North" is not the way of describing Scotland, but referred to the North of England.

Our editor, as the reader by this time knows, has ways of his own, and generally contrives for us a surprise or two. How characteristic that, when collecting all the contemporaneous accounts of Johnson — from Piozzi to "Tom Tyers"—he should designedly omit the most sprightly and artistic record of them all, viz. Miss Burney's! Her sketches are almost as dramatic as Boswell's, and quite as amusing and important too. It is leaving out the part of Hamlet. The editor's reason is extraordinary: "Reflection soon convinced me that it was too good a work *to be hacked in pieces*," which we must suppose is the proper description of the process that has been applied to the other works. This, however, with all respect, does not seem to be the real motive that was working in the editor's mind. To have merely selected the episodes that referred to Johnson would not have been an injury to the work. "It is a great pity that the Diary *has never had a competent editor;* it is not altogether as she wrote it. Surely the original entries might be restored?" And as surely might not the cuttings and extracts from *Ramblers*, Walpole's, etc., be supplied by the same competent editor, to the utter extinction of poor Fanny. At all events, we have here an editor that has omitted from a collection one of its most important and necessary components, in order that it may be later on printed in complete form. What do his publishers say to this?

The editor has a system of making his notes go as far as possible. In the "Letters" there are profuse references to "The Life," and in the "Miscellanies" references as profuse to both preceding works. This may be justified, but not so the system of making a note and text do alternate duty. Thus, in "The Life" we have a passage quoted from the "Letters" as an illustration. When we come to the "Letters," the passage in "The Life" does duty as a note. In the "Miscellanies" we find him actually repeating some of the notes in "The Life": witness that on the "Epilogue to Johnson's Play," where we are told twice over, "the wonder is that Johnson accepted this Epilogue, which is a little coarse and a little profane."

The fashion, indeed, in which the editor tries to "belittle" the sage wherever he can is scarcely decorous. During the Holy Week Johnson wrote in his "Diary" that he had an awe upon him, "not thinking of the Passion till I looked in the Almanac." This natural unaffected confession the editor thus twists: "Apparently *he had omitted Church* of late." How? When? Observe, he had remembered and kept the solemnity, for he states that he fasted from meat and wine. The Almanac had reminded him, and he kept the feasts duly.

Here is another trivial cavil. Johnson penitentially reminds himself that he had spent fifty-five years making resolutions and failing to keep them. The editor notes that he was then fifty-five years old, "so he must have begun making resolutions at the time he was born." This is indeed being literal. But Johnson, to show that he was speaking generally, adds that he had been making resolutions "from the earliest time *almost that I can remember*," and might fairly count it the whole of his life.

It is impossible not to smile over the editor's comical complaint of Mrs Piozzi's behaviour to him. It is quite a penal matter. "The frequent errors of Mrs Piozzi" did not so much affect Boswell or Johnson or herself—no, but "*caused me a great deal of trouble*." Very improper of the lady, no doubt. "Some of them were *clearly intentional;* not a few letters were carelessly inserted in the wrong places, but of her own some *are fabrications*"!

But it is really amazing how the editor's prejudice against Mrs Thrale makes him unconsciously distort. She has always met with harsh treatment in the matter of her second marriage, which was certainly an indiscretion. Of the four or five letters that passed between her and Johnson on the occasion, she thought it advisable to publish only two. The second and third were of too painful and resentful a character to print. The editor charges her with wishing to make Johnson suppose that she was already married, so that his objection would come too late. Nothing can be more unfounded. For she speaks of it as "a connection which he must have heard of from many," that is, an attachment, for the "many" could not have heard of the marriage, and she only concealed it from him, she says, to avoid the pain of rejecting his advice. She tells it to him because "*it is all irrevocably settled*," and out of his power to prevent. Is not this an exact description of an engagement and not of a marriage? But what is conclusive on the point is that with her letter she sends Johnson her circular to the executors, and which bears the *same date* as her letter, viz. June 30. In it she says in plain terms that her daughters, "having heard that Mr Piozzi *is* coming back from Italy, judging that his return *would be succeeded by our marriage*" etc. She even concludes her first letter with "I feel *as if acting without* a parent's consent till you write kindly," etc.—that is, "as if acting," not "as if I had acted," which she would have written had the business been done. And yet the editor contends that she wished to persuade Johnson that she was already married! It is inconceivable how he can fall into such mistakes. It is also urged that she calls Piozzi her husband; and she adds that "the birth of my second husband is not meaner," etc. But there is nothing in the point, as it is plain she means her future husband.

Here is an interesting matter which has escaped the editor. In November 1779, when the Thrales were at Bath, "Queenie" wrote the sage a letter, and Fanny Burney, who was not without her affectations, thought it would be effective to add a little deferential postscript to the child's letter. The doctor was in an ill-humour, and fancied they were beginning to neglect him. "Queenie," he wrote, "sent me a pretty letter, to which . . . added *a silly short note* in such a silly white hand that I was glad it was no longer." This was certainly rough and unmannerly to his favourite, and as she is at once to be recognised from allusions in the "Letters," it seemed strange that Mrs Piozzi should have allowed it to stand. But the fact was that when these "Letters" were published, she was in a bitter mood against Fanny, who had opposed her marriage, and she, no doubt, felt a little malicious satisfaction in letting this thrust stand.

As Mrs Thrale was "a forger and fabricator," so another of the coterie is described as a thief. Mr Seward published a collection in four volumes, called "Anecdotes of Distinguished Persons," a rather entertaining miscellany, containing some 2000 pages, of which three are given to Dr Johnson. In these three pages are found some of Mrs Thrale's anecdotes, and these are "thefts." The editor seems angry because "some of these thefts I only discovered in correcting the proof sheets"—a personal incident that does not concern us. But it touches the editor nearly. "It might be thought that plagiarism such as this would be easily detected *by one who was so familiar with the subject.*" But it was this familiarity which made detection difficult. "Every anecdote I had long known so well I could not be sure," and so on. But the reader has no concern with these thoughts and feelings of Dr B. Hill, whether he saw a thing in the proof or otherwise.

There is a French "Dictionaire Portatif" of one L'Avocat mentioned, of which the editor seriously announces: "This work is not in the British Museum." If this be a reason for its non-existence it will not hold, for there are a east number of books not in the British Museum which do exist. But there *is* there a late edition of the "Dictionaire Portatif," edited by some one else, which is probably the same.

The editor's fashion of assuming as truth whatever his enthusiasm makes him *wish* to be true is shown by the following:—"My kinsman, Mr Horatio Beaumont," possesses a copy of Boswell's "Life," in which are some marginal notes by a nameless writer. The editor, however, believes that they were written by one Mr Hussey, who was a friend of Johnson's. This was fair subject for conjecture. But the editor having decided beyond appeal that they were Hussey's, all through his work always speaks of them as Hussey's marginal notes, and we have, "Mr Hussey says," and "Mr Hussey thinks," although there is not a particle of evidence for giving him the authorship.

Dr B. Hill seems to hold an arbitrary theory that any spinster of the time, when touching on fifty or thereabouts, was summarily compelled to become "Mrs" So-and-so, and to drop her "Miss." There is no foundation for this, save that we find them when grown elderly sometimes addressed as "Mrs."

We are thus assured that Miss Reynolds, Sir Joshua's sister, who was fifty-four years old, "in accordance with the common custom, was now dignified as Mrs Reynolds." Miss Porter, he decides, became of a sudden Mrs Porter. Yet on another occasion, we are told that "though Miss Mulso was but twenty-eight . . . she was complimented with the title of *Mrs* Mulso." At twenty-eight! Where, then, is the editor's "common custom"? And Mrs Carter, who never married, was always known as Mrs Carter. And what of Mrs Hannah More?

Here is a rather startling assertion:—"Johnson, if I am not mistaken, in the frequency with which he is quoted, comes next to the Bible and Shakespeare." Even as it stands, this too sweeping statement fails, for the thousands who readily quote their Shakespeare and Bible never quote anything from Johnson. He is not in popular circulation, as it were. But the writer who is next in demand to the two named is surely Dickens, who has furnished scores of stock phrases, which are in constant use. Not a day passes that we do not see in the papers something of Sam Weller's, or the circumlocution office, the Pickwickian sense, etc.

On the strength of his collection of extracts and snippets, Dr B. Hill proudly claims the title of "scholar," and appeals to fellow-scholars in England and America. These books are far more journalistic than scholar-like, since we have such notes as this mixed up with others on the Johnsonian coterie—"When I had the honour of meeting Mr Gladstone at Oxford on February 6, 1890," etc.; or "When, a few years ago, the Prince of Wales asked General Gordon," etc.

Turning back for a moment to the "Letters," we find Dr B. Hill making a "discovery" or two, on which he claims credit. There is the cancel of a passage in Johnson's "Journey," one which is so creditable to him. He had originally set down a "censure of the clergy of an English Cathedral," accusing them of longing to melt "the lead on the roof, and that it was only just they should swallow what they melted." Our editor found Gough's copy in the Bodleian in which the suppressed passage was written, which he was thus enabled to supply. Alas for the doctor's "discoveries." I have a little book called a "Bibliographical Tour," or some such title, in which the passage is printed, which no doubt Gough copied. The Cathedral was certainly Lichfield, where the roof was actually stripped thirteen years after Johnson wrote. The editor, who is fond of relating the processes of his mind before he arrives at a conclusion, at one time strangely fancied it might have been St Paul's, as though the Dean and Canons would have been permitted to strip off and sell the lead. This notion, however, he dismissed, not because of its ludicrousness, but because he was assured by a certain "Rev W. Sparrow Simpson," "that it was *very improbable* that the Dean and Chapter entertained such an idea," a Bunsby-like verdict, which quite satisfied our editor. First he thought the Dean was Newton, then he was Addenbroke, and so on.

Once writing from Lichfield, in June 21, 1775, a gossiping letter to amuse Mrs Thrale, Johnson said: "They give me good words, and cherries and strawberries. Mrs Cobb is come to Mrs Porter's this afternoon, Miss A—— comes little near me, and everybody talks of you." In these simple sentences the editor discovers "There is an omission here, *as is shown by the structure of the sentence.*" I am certain no one else could discover this from "the structure of the sentence," which is artistic enough of its kind. But what was this omission? A special compliment paid to Mrs Thrale, for she refers to it in her reply. All wrong. We turn to her reply of June 24, and there read: "'Tis very flattering to me when people make my talents the subject of their praises, in order to obtain your favour." Here she refers to Johnson's compliment "every one talks of you." The truth is, the editor is always in a hurry, and, not pausing to consider, was misled by the preceding sentence.

Every one knows Johnson's pleasant "hit" at the attorneys: "He did not care to speak ill of any man behind his back, but he believed the gentleman was an attorney." Mrs Piozzi repeats the same speech, which moves the editor to this indignant burst: "When we see how this sarcasm *has been spoilt* by Mrs Piozzi, we may quote," etc.: that is, Fitzherbert's remark that few persons are capable of "carrying a *bon mot*." Here is the lady's version: "I would be loathe to speak ill of any person who I do not know deserves it, but I am afraid he is an attorney." The only difference is "would be loathe," instead of "did not care," and "I am afraid" instead of "I believe."

Mrs Thrale, on her mother's death, spoke of the touching "spectacle of beauty subdued by disease." "It must have been," says the editor, "a good deal subdued by age, for she was sixty-six." He will not have such things as handsome old or elderly ladies. Yet some of us have seen good-looking old ladies. We may wonder where Dr B. Hill has been living.

One of the most extraordinary questions in the relation of Boswell and Johnson, which was so intimate and lasted so long, the editor has not investigated, or scarcely touched. "Why was not Boswell at Johnson's death-bed?" And, "Why was he not mentioned in Johnson's will?" Both questions are, of course, connected.

It throws further light on Boswell's strangely morbid character, and also upon one of the odd "anfractuosities" of human nature. After expending so much time and labour in waiting on his great friend, it is strange to find him at the very close and crisis foolishly throwing all his exertions to waste, owing to some humour or caprice which he found it impossible to control. In a certain class of character this is not uncommon. Boswell, who was always seeking excuses for coming up to town, ought certainly to have found his way thither after Johnson, in June 1783, had suffered from a paralytic stroke. He allowed nearly a whole year to pass without a visit. Then came the application for the increase of pension to enable Johnson to go abroad. This business was set on foot by Boswell, who applied to the Chancellor about June 20th, but without informing Johnson. Now this was a delicate and rather awkward business, being a plea *in forma pauperis*, and should not have been attempted without judicious approaches and an almost certainty of success. What was so compromising in the matter was that Johnson was not in want of money at all. He had some two thousand pounds put by, and a couple of hundred pounds would have been sufficient for the journey. When he was told of the application, he must have had an uneasy consciousness of all this; the only thing that could salve his scruples was that he had taken no part in the business. But to have it supposed that he had tried to get public money that he was not in want of, and then to fail, was truly mortifying. He must, not unreasonably, have laid it all to "Bozzy's" account, who, moreover, did not bestir himself sufficiently. Instead of waiting in town to look after the matter, Boswell left on the 30th. Johnson seems to have expected him to stay, for he wrote to him, "I wish your affairs could have permitted a longer and continued exertion of your zeal and kindness."

His health now grew worse and worse; but Boswell in his letters, kept "bothering" for his advice about settling in London, etc., always writing, as he says, in bad spirits, with dejection and fretfulness, and at the same time "expressing anxious apprehensions concerning him on *account of a dream*." This, to a man suffering as Johnson was, must have been painful. He wrote back impatiently, chiefly in terms of reproach, "on a supposed charge of affecting discontent and indulging the vanity of complaint." Who could take offence at this, for the sage was miserably ill—dying, in fact. But, he added, "Write to me often, and write like a man. I consider your fidelity and tenderness as a great part of the comforts which are yet left to me." And then he says, "I sincerely wish we could be *nearer* to each other." There are blanks marked by stars both in this and in the preceding letter, which show that the rebukes were so severe that Boswell would not venture to print them. But the sick or dying sage, feeling that he had been a little rough, two days later hastened to make a sort of *amende*, hoping that he would not take it amiss, for it contained only truth, and that kindly intended. It evidently rankled, for Boswell, knowing that the reader is wondering that he did not hurry to his friend, makes this halting explanation: "I unfortunately was so much indisposed during a considerable part of the year, that it was not, or at least, *I thought it was not*, in my power" —not to take a journey or leave home—but "*to write to my illustrious friend as formerly, or without expressing such complaints as offended him.*" A most extraordinary "compulsion to silence" this! But his next proceeding was more singular still. Conjuring him "*not to do me the injustice of charging me with affectation*," thus anticipating further quarrel, he came to the formal resolution of taking no further notice of his dying friend. "I was with much regret long silent," and for *three months* not a line came from him. Johnson, who was within six weeks of his death, in vain wrote to him kindly and tenderly, describing his own wretched state, and saying that Boswell's letters were a comfort. "Are you sick, or are you sullen?" he asked. The morbid Boswell, however, could nurse his grievances: "It was painful to me to find that *he still persevered in arraigning me as before*, which was strange in him who had so much experience of what I had suffered." This shows clearly that he was trying to throw the blame on Johnson, and thus show that it was the ill-humour of the testator that caused his exclusion from the will. At last, with a great effort, Boswell forced himself to write, "two as kind letters as I could," one of which was dated in the first week of November, the second about six weeks later. This arrived, however, when Johnson was actually dying, and could not be read by him. Can we wonder, therefore, that Johnson was deeply offended by such neglect, and that he left the name of Boswell out of his will.

The latter must have been deeply mortified, as he knew what malicious remarks would be made on the omission. There were memorials left to all the intimate friends, Hawkins, Langton, Reynolds, Dr Scott, Windham, Strahan, the four doctors, Gerard Hamilton, Miss Reynolds, the two Hooles, Desmoulins, Sastres, and Mrs Gardiner, the tallow chandler! But not even a book to Boswell. Nothing could be more deliberate or more pointed. Boswell very feebly urges, and he had better have passed over the matter, that Johnson had also omitted many of his friends, such as Murphy, Adams, Taylor, Dr Burney, Hector, and "the author of this work." But none of these except Taylor and Boswell could be placed in the same category with those named in the will.

On the whole of this curious episode, Dr B. Hill has nothing to contribute save a far-fetched theory, that Johnson only named such friends as he *saw*, and whose presence therefore was a reminder. Yet he saw his old favourite "Queenie" Thrale, and made no mention of her. Gerard Hamilton was not with him, yet he mentioned him. Burke was sitting with him, and attending him, yet he was not mentioned. Like the editor's other theories this one will not hold.*

There are some oddities in the arrangement of the volumes. It seems "a freak," for instance, the placing the index not at the end, but before a portion of the text. Having done with the index, we begin again with what is oddly called—by another freak—"A Concordance of Johnson's Sayings." Now, as Dr B. Hill might learn from the Oxford Dictionary, a concordance means "a citation of parallel passages in a book," or as in the case of the Gospels, "a book which shows in how many texts of Scripture any word occurs," a definition which *is* in Johnson's Dictionary. The editor's description is, therefore, meaningless. To our surprise, however, we find at the beginning of the volumes another batch of Johnson's sayings, entitled "Johnson's apothegms, opinions, etc." Surely these ought to be in the misnamed "Concordance." This specimen, however, is a fair illustration of the methods of our mercurial editor.

And now, having made these serious charges, and having given good evidences for them, I think it is incumbent on Dr B. Hill to come out "into the open," and defend his edi-

---

* Since the former portions of this Examination were printed, I have been informed, on good authority, that the lady who refused the editor admission to Auchinleck is not dead, as I stated she was.

tions. It will not exactly do, ostrich-like, to hide his head in the sands of the Clarendon Press. I think he is required to stand forth and vindicate himself, or confess his errors. It will not do, as he has done in these "miscellanies," to print declarations of Dr Johnson—obviously to *my* address—that attacks need not be noticed, etc. When Boswell pleaded to his father that Homer nodded, the old judge said—" But you're not Homer," and Dr B. Hill is not exactly Dr Johnson.

I must now conclude this "Critical Examination," adding that I have refrained from inserting many more passages to which exception might justly be taken, but which are not of so "telling" a class as those selected. Apart from the innumerable mistakes pointed out, it has been shown that these abundantly noted books are not *editions* of Boswell, Johnson, or the other folk—but simply "encyclopædias of anecdotes," copied with much diligence from all quarters—and so far are entertaining.

Nor are the syndics of the Clarendon Press without their share of responsibility. They have professed to furnish purchasers with "editions" of the works in question, and, instead, have supplied a heterogeneous mass of details about everybody and everything. Nearly a century ago, they sent forth a fine edition of Boswell's work, in four volumes, beautifully printed, a fine specimen of reserve in the matter of editing; what will they do now?

It will be noted that no references to the passages quoted are furnished in this "Critical Examination," for, with the aid of the editor's copious indexes, they can be found at once.

www.ingramcontent.com/pod-product-compliance
Lightning Source LLC
Chambersburg PA
CBHW020037030726
47499CB00007B/2474

* 9 7 8 3 3 3 7 3 9 8 7 0 5 *